THE MAN IN THE DARK

In Burma, the British manager of the ruby mines of Mogok has been away, attempting to track down a leopard that had been attacking livestock. He returns to discover his stand-in at the office lying dead on the floor, the safe door open and its contents stolen. Fifty of the mine's finest rubies had been awaiting shipment to the company's London office. Those jewels, seemingly endowed with evil powers, are destined to cause numerous men to meet their deaths . . .

DONALD STUART

THE MAN IN THE DARK

Complete and Unabridged

LINFORD
Leicester

First published in Great Britain

First Linford Edition
published 2013

Copyright © 1935 by Gerald Verner
Copyright © 2012 by Chris Verner

British Library CIP Data

Stuart, Donald.
 The man in the dark. - -
 (Linford mystery library)
 1. Mogok (Burma)- -Fiction.
 2. Detective and mystery stories.
 3. Large type books.
 I. Title II. Series
 823.9'2–dc23

 ISBN 978–1–4448–1474–3

Published by
F. A. Thorpe (Publishing)
Anstey, Leicestershire

Set by Words & Graphics Ltd.
Anstey, Leicestershire
Printed and bound in Great Britain by
T. J. International Ltd., Padstow, Cornwall

This book is printed on acid-free paper

Prologue

Robbery and Tragedy

Malcolm Graeme, the British manager of the famous Ruby Mines of Mogok, in the wilds of Upper Burma, rose at early dawn, hurriedly pulled on his clothes and stepped out to the veranda of his bungalow on the hillside.

There was a strained look on his face. Eagerly, with a vague feeling of dread, he gazed down the valley, over the tangled, twisted growth of jungle, to the straggling little town of Mogok; gazed with keen eyes and listening intently, apprehensive of hearing a faint clamour of alarm, or of seeing somebody hastening up the hill to bring him bad news.

But all was quiet and peaceful. He heard only the twittering of birds, and saw only the dim figures of natives moving to their daily toil.

'There can't be anything wrong,' he said to himself. 'It was stupid of me to get such an idea into my head.'

He was greatly relieved. The shadow that had haunted him was gone. During the previous day he had tramped for miles in the jungle, vainly trying to find the trail of a leopard which had been lurking in the neighbourhood and had killed a couple of goats; and coming back to his bungalow after sunset, weary and hungry, he had snatched a bite of food, and turned in for the night.

Tired as he was, though, he had tossed restlessly on his bed until nearly morning, his brain active from worry; and he had been on the point of rising and going down to the mine buildings, when he finally dropped off to sleep.

Under ordinary circumstances he would not have been in the least uneasy. It was his habit to sleep in the bungalow, and his trusted clerk, Neil Allison, always slept in one of the offices of the company.

In this instance, however, there had

been three reasons for Malcolm Graeme's anxiety. In the first place, he had on the previous morning, before departing on his quest, given the key of the safe to Neil Allison.

In the second place, while searching for the leopard, he had fallen in with two Britishers whose appearance he did not like, and he had not been entirely satisfied with the account they gave of themselves, plausible as it was.

And in the third place, there was at this time, in the office safe, a parcel of fifty of the largest and choicest rubies the mines of Mogok had ever yielded. They had been accumulating, and were shortly to be sent to the company's head offices in London by way of the Irrawaddy River and Rangoon.

Sifted out from smaller stones, and from the refuse of the mines — flakes of sapphire and amethyst and topaz — these big rubies were absolutely flawless; they were of the purest pigeon-blood red, and they were worth about four thousand pounds each.

It was little wonder, then, that Malcolm

Graeme had been uneasy. But, fortunately, there had been no ground for his fears. Nothing could have happened to interfere with his plans, to prevent him from taking his six months' leave of absence in England, where his daughter was living with an aunt. He had been looking forward to it with the happiest of anticipations, and he was to start on the morrow.

He had a good appetite for the breakfast his native servant laid for him on the veranda, and the sun was not yet above the horizon when he left the bungalow, and walked down the winding path, and across a strip of dusty white road to the edge of the picturesque little town, where stood the building of the mining company.

To his surprise, there was no sign of life here. Where was the clerk? He should have been up and about at this hour.

Malcolm Graeme's apprehensions returned. Finding the outer door locked, he rapped on it loudly, and called at the top of his voice. There was no answer. He could not hear any movement within.

Now certain that something was seriously wrong, he wrenched the door from its fastenings by a single heave of his shoulder, and pitched reeling into the front office. A glance showed him that no one was here.

He hurried to a door at the farther end of the room, and forced that open also; and as he looked beyond him, into the private office, a cry of horror burst from his lips.

His worst fears had been realized. Stark tragedy met his eyes. He stared at an open window — at the open safe by the wall — at the huddled, motionless figure of Neil Allison.

The young man lay on the floor, cold in death, killed by a crushing blow on the head. Close to him was a dagger with a crudely engraved hilt, and tightly clenched in one of his hands was a ragged strip of crimson cloth, which had obviously been torn from a native kummerbund.

Scattered around him were a number of sapphires and amethysts, and small rubies of insignificant value. But where was the pouch of black velvet — the pouch containing the big rubies that were worth two hundred thousand pounds?

It was not here. It was not in the safe. Those wonderful stones, the finest the mines had ever yielded, had been stolen. It was a stupendous loss.

As he grasped the full nature of the calamity, as he thought of the consequences that might result from it, Malcolm Graeme pressed his hands to his throbbing temples, and groaned in anguish of mind. He would be blamed, of course; and perhaps he would lose his berth, be dismissed in disgrace.

Yes, it would come to that. He had encountered those two strange Britishers of forbidding appearance, and having reason to suspect they were in the neighbourhood for no good purpose, he should have slept in the office with the clerk last night, instead of at his bungalow. If only he had done so!

He pulled himself together, and tried to think clearly. Were his suspicions wrong?

What of the dagger, and the strip of cloth in Neil Allison's hand? They indicated that the murderers, who had got in by the window, belonged to the notorious Boh Thaw's band of dacoits, who had for years been a menace to Upper Burma.

Could that theory be entertained? No, it was most improbable. The dagger and the torn kummerbund had been left here as a blind, to put the police on a false scent. There had been no news of Boh Thaw for several months, since he had been reported to be in the mountainous region at the headwaters of the Irrawaddy River. Furthermore, he and his band had always confined their operations to killing and robbing travellers on the jungle roads.

Malcolm Graeme shook his head. 'Those Britishers are the guilty parties,' he reflected. 'There can't be any doubt of it. Every effort must be made to trace them. I am afraid, though, they have fled into the wild country towards the Siamese frontier.'

He thoroughly searched the room, and, not having discovered anything that would confirm his theory, he hastened from the building, and walked rapidly through the town.

He would report the murder and robbery at the barracks. Then he would get his horse and ride into the jungle to find a man who, he believed, would be able to give valuable assistance to the police. And that man was no other than Lionel Crane, the famous detective.

II

In the Jungle

More than once, in the course of the travels Lionel Crane's calling entailed on him, demands had been made on his professional skill. In this instance the Government had lent him out to Rangoon on a secret mission, and having brought his task to a satisfactory conclusion, he and Harry Pollard, his young partner, had gone up to Mogok to visit Crane's old friend, Captain Murdoch, the District Superintendent of Police.

They had stayed there for a short time, and then, accompanied by the captain and half a dozen native porters, they had gone into the jungle, and pitched a camp three or four miles to the east of the ruby mines, in the hope of enjoying a memorable safari.

That was nearly a week ago, and as yet they had not had any luck in spotting any tigers, seeing only a panther, and a couple of leopards; and they were about to set forth again on the morning after the robbery, when Malcolm Graeme rode at a gallop into the camp, and threw himself from his lathered horse.

'Thank heaven you are still here!' he exclaimed. 'I was afraid you had moved on, and I wouldn't be able to find you! I have the worst of news! Murder and robbery at the mines, Murdoch! Neil Allison was killed last night, and the great rubies were stolen from the office safe! I hope Mr. Crane will help you to find the thieves! If the rubies are not recovered it will be a very serious thing for me! I may lose my berth!'

Captain Murdoch looked staggered. Crane nodded gravely. The big rubies had been shown to him, and he knew their value.

Continuing, Malcolm Graeme told of his discoveries that morning, speaking in an agitated voice; and then he mentioned the two Britishers he had met on the previous day, describing them as crafty-looking individuals of middle-age.

'I took an instinctive aversion to them,' he said, 'though they spoke like educated men. I ran across them in a lonely part of the jungle less than a mile from Mogok, and questioned them closely. They gave the names of John Burnley and George Harrap. They had a camp in the vicinity, they stated, and they were drawing maps of the district for a firm of London cartographers. It was a queer story, and I was not inclined to believe it.'

Captain Murdoch shrugged his shoulders.

'Very queer,' he assented. 'I don't doubt they are the guilty parties. The crime could not have been committed by any of the natives employed at the mines — they are all trustworthy — and Boh Thaw and his band of dacoits are also beyond suspicion. But don't take it so hard, Graeme. They can't blame you in the least.'

'I am afraid they will,' Malcolm Graeme gloomily answered. 'Knowing those men were in the neighbourhood, I ought to have slept in the office with Allison last night.'

'Well, don't worry. I dare say it won't be long until the thieves have been caught. We will send telegrams down country.'

'Down country? They wouldn't be so stupid as to go in that direction. They will probably try to get over the border into Siam.'

Crane questioned the disconsolate manager.

'Did you find any fingerprints in the office?' he asked.

'There are none at all,' Malcolm Graeme replied. 'I made a thorough search.'

'How was the safe opened? By force?'

'No, Mr. Crane. The clerk's key was in the lock. It had been taken from his pocket.'

'How much of a start do you suppose the murderers got?'

'I don't know. I can only tell you that poor Allison's body was quite cold when I found him.'

'Cold, was it? Then we can safely presume that it was soon after or before midnight when — '

Crane paused abruptly, and lifted a warning finger.

'Somebody is coming this way,' he whispered.

All were silent, listening to heavy, floundering steps that were approaching. They stopped, came on, and stopped again. The person appeared to be in distress. He drew nearer and nearer, with unsteady tread, and of a sudden he burst out from the edge of the green cover — a tall man of perhaps forty, with a fair moustache and beard.

He stood still for a moment, staring at the little group, seemingly inclined to turn back. Then he staggered forward into the camp, pausing for breath, and leaned limply against a tree.

He was bareheaded, and ghastly white. His clothes had been torn by thorny bushes, and a bloodstained handkerchief was bound loosely around his left arm above the elbow.

'Dacoits!' he gasped. 'Dacoits! Last night!'

Malcolm Graeme clutched him by the shoulder.

13

'This is one of the scoundrels who murdered my clerk and stole the rubies, Mr. Crane!' he cried. 'This is the one who gave the name of John Burnley!'

The man shook his head.

'You are wrong!' he declared. 'I am as innocent as you are!'

'It's no use denying your guilt!' Malcolm Graeme exclaimed. 'Where is your accomplice? Where are the rubies?'

'I — I haven't got them! If you will let me explain — '

'The rubies, you villain! Where are they? You must know something about them, from what you have said.'

'Yes, I knew they had been stolen. But I had nothing to do with that, nor had my friend Harrap.'

'It is a lie! Confess at once, or I will — '

Captain Murdoch interfered. He calmed the angry manager, and at a word or two from Crane the suspected man began his story.

'Our camp was close to a jungle trail,' he said, 'and it was a couple of hours after midnight, as nearly as I can judge, when George Harrap and I were roused by footsteps and voices. A number of people were coming towards us. We supposed they were dacoits, and they were already so close that we would have been heard if we had taken to flight. So we remained perfectly still, hoping we would not be discovered. Our fire had burnt very low, and gave only a feeble glimmer of light.

'We had a dim glimpse of the men through a fringe of bushes. There were about a score of them, evil-looking fellows, armed to the teeth. They were talking as they approached, and we heard them speak of rubies they had stolen. As they were passing by, our fire suddenly burst into flames, and the dacoits saw us, and attacked us at once. I fired my pistol as they rushed into the camp, and I think I shot two of them.

'What happened next is almost a blank to me. My pistol was knocked from my grasp, and I was slashed on the arm with a sword. I remember seeing Harrap struggling with four or five of the natives, and as I could do nothing for him, I took to my heels, and got away. I was pursued by some of the dacoits, but they lost sight of me in the darkness, and turned back. I lost my bearings afterwards. I have been wandering about for hours, and it was by chance that I stumbled on your camp. As for Harrap, I don't know if he is dead or alive. I am afraid he was killed.'

It was a straightforward story John Burnley had told. Was it true, or had he and his companion stolen the rubies, and been subsequently attacked by the dacoits, who had been lurking in the vicinity of Mogok? Captain Murdoch was inclined to believe the tale, and so was Malcolm Graeme.

'It looks as if my suspicions were wrong,' he said sadly. 'The dacoits are the thieves, and it is not likely they will be caught. I shall be held responsible for the loss of the rubies.'

'Yes, Graeme, it appears you were wrong,' assented the captain. 'If this man and his companion were the thieves, they would hardly have gone to sleep in their camp. They would have put as many miles as possible between them and the mines.'

Crane was not satisfied. Though John

Burnley was an entire stranger to him, he strongly suspected that he was a crook. He might be able to identify him, he reflected, with his beard and moustache off. He searched the man, and found only a pipe and a tobacco-pouch, and a considerable sum of money.

'Is Burnley your real name?' he inquired.

'Yes, it is,' was the answer. 'I was born in London, and I have always lived there.'

'In what part?'

'I had chambers in the West End. I have a private income.'

'You told Mr. Graeme that you and your friend Harrap were drawing maps of the district for a London firm of cartographers. Was that true?'

'No, it was not.'

'Indeed? Why did you lie?'

'Harrap and I were afraid of getting into trouble. We came to Burma to shoot elephants, and we had no licences. We have not even seen an elephant, though, so we haven't broken the law.'

'I think I have seen you somewhere before,' Crane continued, untruthfully. 'I am Lionel Crane, the private detective.'

John Burnley's countenance did not change.

'I have heard of you, of course,' he quietly replied, 'but I have no recollection of ever seeing you, sir.'

'Have you and your friend been to the mines of Mogok since you came to Burma?'

'No; we gave the place a wide berth, not having game licences.'

'Yet you camped in the vicinity of the town. How was that?'

'We were in a lonely part of the jungle. We thought we were safe from discovery there.'

'You were in the same camp last night?'

'The same one, sir.'

'You could find the way to it?'

'Yes, very easily,' the man answered, without hesitation.

'Very well, you shall take us there,' said Crane. 'If there are any dead dacoits at the camp, Murdoch,' he added, 'we will be the more inclined to believe this fellow's story.'

III

An Unsolved Mystery

John Burnley had been utterly exhausted when he arrived at the camp, but a hearty meal and a stiff drink of brandy pulled him together. His wounded arm was dressed and bandaged and he set off with Crane and Pollard, Captain Murdoch and Malcolm Graeme, the native porters remaining behind.

The direction taken was to the north-east, and a rapid march of about five miles, under John Burnley's guidance — he had no difficulty in finding the way by daylight — brought the party to the spot where the two men had been attacked.

Dacoits had been here. There could be no mistake about that. The confused footprints of natives shod with sandals were visible on the jungle path and in the camp itself.

And by the cold ashes of the fire lay the dead bodies of two men — lean, little brown men with brutal features, clad in cotton tunics and drawers and scarlet kummerbunds. One had been shot in the head, the other in the chest.

'These fellows belonged to Boh Thaw's band,' declared Captain Murdoch. 'There can't be any doubt of it.'

Malcolm Graeme nodded.

'The scoundrels are getting bolder,' he said. 'I am amazed that they should have the audacity to rob the company. And of rubies! Heretofore they have only murdered travellers for their money and firearms.'

Crane shrugged his shoulders.

'I don't see any of your belongings here, Burnley,' he remarked.

'The dacoits carried everything off naturally,' John Burnley replied.

'What did you have?'

'A full outfit, sir. Rifles and ammunition, blankets, a supply of food, and spare clothes in rucksacks.'

'And what of the rubies?' Crane sharply asked. 'Were they in your friend's possession?'

John Burnley looked him straight in the eyes.

'If that is meant for a joke, sir,' he answered, without the quiver of a muscle, 'it is a very poor one. I have told you I had nothing to do with the robbery, and I told you only the truth. You have no reason to doubt it.'

'I am not saying you are guilty. I have an open mind at present.'

'You are not convinced of my innocence, then?'

'I am not convinced one way or the other, Burnley. Perhaps I will be able to express an opinion before the day is over.'

Captain Murdoch and Malcolm Graeme glanced in surprise at Crane. He stepped out from the glade to the path, and came back in a few moments.

'The man Harrap is alive and a prisoner,' he said. 'I can distinguish his footprints from those of the natives. We may be able to overtake them. There is a chance of it, though I fear it is a very slim one. Come, let us be on the way.'

'You think Harrap may have the rubies?' asked Malcolm Graeme, in a low tone.

'It is possible,' Crane replied. 'It is a mysterious affair, and I don't know what to think as yet.'

The ground was soft and damp, as there had been rain on the previous day, and it was an easy matter to follow the trail of Boh Thaw and his band of marauders.

Crane went in front with Pollard, and Captain Murdoch and Malcolm Graeme brought up the rear with John Burnley, and kept a watchful eye on him, ready to frustrate any attempt at escape.

For hour after hour the party pressed steadily on, holding their course to the east, threading a dense and tangled jungle, seeing at intervals the prints of boots amongst the other footprints. George Harrap was still alive. He had not been put to death by his captors.

Finally, when a distance of five or six miles had been laboriously covered, the trail descended a hill, and wound through a belt of reeds to the bank of a deep and sluggish river.

And that was the end of it. There were no footprints to right or left, but at the edge of the water, bitten into the earth, were marks that told a plain tale.

'Look!' exclaimed Captain Murdoch, in a tone of dismay. 'There have been three or four boats here!'

'Yes, that is obvious,' Crane answered. 'The dacoits probably went up or down the stream.'

'Or they may have crossed to the opposite shore. If so, the boats are hidden amongst the reeds.'

'It would not be safe for us to swim over, Murdoch?'

'No, there are crocodiles in the river.'

Malcolm Graeme's features twitched painfully.

'I shall never see the rubies again!' he said. 'I am a ruined man!'

The dacoits might or might not have committed the robbery and murder at the mines. There was no certainty of it. Be that as it may, they had kidnapped a Britisher; and it could not be doubted that, from fear of the consequences, they would seek refuge in the jungles of Siam or in the mountain fastnesses of northern Burma, where they would be safe from pursuit.

Boh Thaw and his band had a score of hiding places, and it would be useless to send soldiers to search for them. As for George Harrap, he would have to be left to his fate. He might be kept in captivity, but more likely he would be put to death.

Crane and his companions turned back, disappointed by their failure. They did not return to the camp. They went straight to Mogok, which was wildly excited over the crime; and, in spite of his indignant protests, John Burnley was given into the charge of the police, and was lodged in a cell, to be held temporarily on suspicion.

Crane, keenly interested in the case, made a most thorough investigation, and was completely baffled. He found no fingerprints in the room where Neil Allison had been murdered, nor did he discover any footprints in the vicinity of the office building.

His widespread inquiries were fruitless. No one in the town, it appeared, had noticed any suspicious persons on the night of the murder. John Burnley's beard and moustache were shaved off, and the result was disappointing to Crane, who could not identify him as any crook he had known in London.

The man was interrogated again and again, put through a severe cross-examination. But the efforts to trip him up failed.

He stuck to his story, and doggedly, calmly asserted his innocence; and in the end, as there was not a shred of evidence against him, he was set at liberty.

Crane was no wiser than he had been before, and it was with an open mind, not knowing what to believe, that he left the mines with Pollard, and travelled down country on his way back to England. In all likelihood, he felt, the mystery would never be solved.

He was wrong, however. In the near future the trail of the stolen rubies was to cross his path, and lead him ultimately, at peril of his life, to the last scene of the drama on which the curtain had risen in the wilds of Burma.

1

The Hidden Listener

The March night had fallen dark and cold, with a gusty wind driving broken wracks of clouds across the sky, when a big vessel, which had come from the Far East steamed slowly up the Thames, and was made fast at a wharf below London Bridge.

A single passenger came ashore — it was a cargo boat — descending the gangway with a furtive, alert manner, as if he feared there might be some undesirable person waiting to meet him.

He paused for a moment, throwing a sweeping glance around him; and then, his anxiety relieved, he glided away into the darkness, and went through a narrow passage that led him from the wharf to Lower Thames Street.

He was a tall man of middle-age, with a fair moustache, and a complexion that was burnt to a ruddy brown by the sun. He had no luggage. He wore a tweed cap, and his hands were thrust into the pockets of a shaggy jacket, which had obviously not been cut by any English tailor.

He shivered in the biting wind, for, though he was warmly enough clad for even a cold March, he had been for many weeks past in a tropical climate.

He was really glad to be back in London again, yet he was not sure if he would be safe here. He believed he would be, however, if he could disappear into the great city without being followed, and that was all he thought of now.

Still haunted by vague apprehensions, he looked frequently behind him as he trudged up King William Street, stopping at a public house on the way to drink some brandy; and when at length he reached the Bank, and got into a west-bound bus, he was certain he had not been shadowed.

'I hadn't any reason to be worried,' he said to himself. 'No matter what Lionel Crane may have suspected, he couldn't have taken the trouble to keep track of my movements after they set me free, else he or somebody else would have been waiting for the boat.'

Though that fear was gone now — the fear of being kept under surveillance — there were other things to prey on the mind of this man from the Far East.

He had come back almost penniless, cheated by unkind fate out of a share of a rich prize; and there was not a chance in a million, he felt, that he would find in London the accomplice who had been in possession of the proceeds of a robbery.

Moreover, even if by a remote possibility, as by a miracle, that person should be found, he would in all likelihood have returned with empty pockets.

There was no hope in the man's heart, but none the less, when he got out of the bus at the Tottenham Court Road, he struck briskly down into the Soho quarter, and bent his steps to a place where he had been in the habit of going with his friend. This was the Café Spartos, a den of ill-repute, situated in

Bateman Street, between Frith Street and Dean Street.

It might tie imprudent to show himself here, the man reflected as he stopped on the pavement. For a moment he stood there, wavering, and then he went boldly in.

The proprietor, a Greek, gazed at him in surprise, gave him a nod of recognition, and nodded again; The second nod seemed to convey a subtle meaning to the man, and, wondering if the impossible could have happened, he passed through an outer room where a number of people were drinking and smoking, and entered a room at the rear that was curtained off from the café.

It was a small room, comfortably furnished, with couches by the walls. There was only one person here: a dark, well-dressed man, clean-shaven, who was seated at a table with a cigar in his mouth, and a bottle of wine and a glass in front of him.

He stared at the man with the moustache and changed colour; rose to his feet, and held out his hand.

'By Jove, it's Burnley!' he murmured, under his breath.

The other gripped the offered hand.

'Harrap!' he exclaimed, in a low voice. 'By all that's marvellous! I can hardly believe my eyes! You in London, and at the old place!'

'You thought I had been murdered by those yellow scoundrels, of course.'

'I hadn't much doubt of it, Harrap. At all events, I never expected to see you again.'

'Well, I am as much surprised to see you.'

'How is that? Wasn't there anything in the London papers about me?'

'Yes, there was. I knew you had been arrested on suspicion, but I didn't know you had been released. Or did you break gaol?'

'No; they had to let me go. They hadn't any evidence to hold me on.'

The two sat down to the table, and George Harrap had a waiter fetch another glass from the outer room. He filled it with wine, and produced a cigar-case.

'Have a smoke and a drink,' he bade.

John Burnley nodded.

'I've been starving for both,' he answered. 'The stuff they had on the ship was rotten, and the tobacco was as bad.'

He was burning to ask a question, but he shrank from putting it. If he was to be disappointed in the end, let him cling to a ray of hope for a little while. And some hope he had, observing that his friend looked to be in prosperous circumstances, and that he had ordered a wine of an expensive brand.

'I wonder if you are glad to see me?' he said, as he lit a cigar.

'Glad to see you?' George Harrap repeated. 'Why not?'

'I imagined your welcome was a bit chilly.'

'Nonsense, old chap! I've been worrying about you all the time. But let us have your yarn now, from the point where they set you free. I know the rest. It was in the papers — how you blundered into Lionel Crane's camp, and went in pursuit of the dacoits with him, and were afterwards arrested. You were damned lucky to get off.'

'They hadn't a scrap of evidence, as I told you before,' said John Burnley. 'As soon as I was free I got down to Rangoon, and crossed the Bay of Bengal to Calcutta. I was unfortunate there. I was robbed of nearly all my money in a gambling den, and had to work at the docks for several weeks before I saved enough to buy a passage on a tramp steamer. It was bound for the Thames and I landed at London Bridge this evening. That is my story. How long have you been back?'

'For about ten days,' George Harrap replied.

'Did the dacoits let you go?'

'No fear! They would have murdered me if I hadn't escaped. I gave them the slip the night after I was captured, while they were all asleep. I wandered about in the jungle for three or four days, and I was almost starved when, as luck would have it, I hit the Government motoring road to Bangkok, in Siam, just as a car with some tourists came along. I pitched them a plausible tale, and they gave me a lift to Bangkok. From there I travelled by rail to Penang, in Malaya, took a boat to Singapore, and sailed for England on a fast steamer.'

'I suppose you had plenty of money, Harrap?'

'Enough to see me through and a decent amount over. I had an easier time of it than you had. You are broke, I dare say.'

'Stony broke. I'll have to rely on you.'

There was a short silence. George Harrap did not speak. John Burnley looked him straight in the eyes.

'What — what of the rubies?' he asked, in a tense voice.

For an instant George Harrap hesitated.

'I have them,' he replied.

'By jove, really?'

'Yes; the dacoits didn't find them. They were in my boots, with my money.'

'That's the best of news. I didn't expect to hear it. Where are the stones now?'

'At my lodgings, so snugly hidden that no one could possibly find them.'

'You haven't disposed of any of them, Harrap?'

'Not yet. I didn't dare to, as the rubies were fully described in the London papers. We'll have to keep them for a while.'

'How much do you think we will get for them in the end?'

'A little more than half of what they are worth, Burnley. Perhaps one hundred and twenty thousand pounds.'

'Ah, that will be a fortune between us! Meanwhile, you can let me have some money?'

'I can spare you a few pounds,' said George Harrap. 'I am in pretty low water myself. By the way, I want to know how we stand. Did Lionel Crane suspect that you and I stole the rubies?'

'He had his suspicions at first,' John Burnley answered. 'As far as I could judge he believed my story afterwards, though.'

'And the police? And the manager of the mines?'

'I think they were satisfied that the dacoits were the guilty parties.'

'I dare say they did. But I am a trifle uneasy about Lionel Crane. He isn't a man to be easily deceived. I hope you weren't shadowed after you landed this evening.'

'I am certain I was not. I was on my guard.'

George Harrap's troubled countenance brightened.

'Well, that's all right, then,' he said. 'We haven't anything to fear. And now we'll be moving along, Burnley,' he added. 'I will take you to my lodgings after we have had dinner somewhere.'

They finished the wine, rose from the table, and departed. And a few moments later the door of another but smaller apartment, at the rear of the room, was opened, and a man stepped from it.

He was a tall, slim man of about forty, very well dressed, of aristocratic appearance, with a dark moustache that was waxed at the ends, and a pointed tuft of beard on his chin.

He had been playing a cunning game. Night after night for a week, with the connivance of the proprietor of the café, he had been concealed there, while George Harrap sat near him.

35

From his hiding place he had patiently watched and waited, in the hope that a certain event that he vaguely anticipated might occur. And at last his patience had been rewarded. Tonight he had learned what he had been so anxious to know.

'Hungry wolves prey on their kind,' he murmured, with a humorous smile, as he went through to the front room. 'It is the law of self-preservation.'

He nodded significantly to Spartos, passed out to the street, and screwed a monocle into his eye as he strolled away in the darkness of the night.

2

The Man With the Monocle

Lionel Crane had been back in England for a couple of months when, one morning, he drove westward in a taxi on his way to visit Malcolm Graeme.

The manager's worst fears had been realized. Shortly after the news of the robbery and murder at the mines of Mogok had reached the head offices of the company, he had been summoned to London by cablegram. He had told his story, concealing nothing; and the general manager, holding him to be in a measure to blame for what had occurred, had dismissed him from his position and retired him on a meagre pension, with the understanding that he would be reinstated in the event of the stolen rubies being recovered.

He was living with his daughter, and Crane had twice been to see him, to try to cheer him up. On this occasion, however, he had received a brief letter asking him to call. For what reason he did not know.

The cab turned off the Hammersmith Road, in the direction of the river, and presently stopped in front of a modest dwelling that was in a street of cheap villas.

Mary Graeme, a pretty girl of eighteen, opened the door, and took the detective through to a small room.

Malcolm Graeme was here, sitting in an armchair by the window. His disgrace, which he felt keenly, had aged him, broken him down. The last time Crane had seen him he had been in low spirits, but today he appeared to be more cheerful.

'It was very good of you to come, Crane,' he said, as he offered his hand. 'Excuse me if I don't rise. I have a touch of rheumatism.'

'I am sorry to hear it,' Crane replied, as he sat down. 'I hope you will soon be better.'

'I dare say I shall. It is the damp, cold weather. I am not used to the English climate.'

'It is very different from Burma, Graeme.'

'Vastly different. I wish I was back there and perhaps I will be before long.'

'You have heard that you may be reinstated?'

'Not that. But I have hopes. I have made a most significant discovery. That is why I wrote to you. I have seen — '

Malcolm Graeme broke off, his eyes sparkling.

'I ran across one of the two men I saw in the Burmese jungle,' he continued.

Crane nodded.

'I am not surprised,' he said. 'I took it for granted that John Burnley had returned to London after his release.'

'But I don't mean John Burnley.'

'Not — not Harrap?'

'Yes, George Harrap.'

Crane gave a quick start.

'Is it possible?' he exclaimed. 'The man who was carried off by the dacoits?'

'The same,' Malcolm Graeme declared. 'I recalled him clearly. It was yesterday afternoon. I went up to the West End on business, and I was walking along

Piccadilly when George Harrap passed me. He was clean-shaven, as he was when I saw him in Burma.'

'It is almost incredible. I think you must have been mistaken.'

'I am certain I was not. I could swear to his identity, Crane.'

'He saw you?'

'No, he did not even glance at me.'

'Did you follow him, Graeme?'

'I tried to, but I lost sight of him in the crowd. He was going towards Piccadilly Circus.'

'Was he alone?' asked Crane. 'Or was Burnley with him?'

'Not Burnley,' Malcolm Graeme replied. 'He was with another man.'

'Another man. What was he like? Give me as accurate a description of him as you can.'

'He was a tall, slim man of middle-age, fashionably dressed, and of very respectable appearance. He had a black moustache waxed at the ends, and a tuft of pointed beard on his chin. And he wore a monocle.'

Crane gave another quick start.

'The man you have described,' he said,

in a tense voice, 'answers perfectly to the description of Edgar Creed.'

'Edgar Creed?' repeated Malcolm Graeme. 'Who is he?'

'A notorious but gentlemanly crook. A suave, cunning, dangerous man. He has served several terms of penal servitude, but he is not wanted for anything by the police at present. He has not long been out of Dartmoor. I had a glimpse of him a few days ago, and he was just as you have described him — waxed moustache, tuft of beard, and monocle.'

'And he was with George Harrap! It looks very suspicious, doesn't it?'

'It is more than suspicious. Much more.'

'I think so myself, Crane. Do you believe, from the fact of George Harrap being with this crook, that it was he and Burnley who murdered young Allison and stole the rubies?'

'In all likelihood. I strongly believe that now, though I had doubts as to their guilt before.'

'Then Harrap probably brought the rubies back with him from Burma, and if so there is a chance of their being recovered.'

'Yes, if he brought them to England. But he may have been robbed of them by the dacoits. There is no certainty of it, however. At all events, Graeme, you must not be too hopeful.'

So George Harrap, the companion of John Burnley, had contrived to escape from the clutches of Boh Thaw and his band, and was here in London! There was a glitter in Crane's eyes. He had doubted the guilt of the two men, as he had just remarked; but there was little or no doubt in his mind now. He had picked up, thousands of miles away from Burma, the broken threads of the ruby mines mystery. To what would they lead him?

'There are obvious deductions to be drawn,' he said, 'starting with Edgar Creed. He is a crook, and an ex-convict. He keeps company only with his own kind. That he should be on friendly terms with George Harrap clearly indicates that Harrap also is a crook, and, that being the case, it is to be presumed that he and Burnley stole the rubies, and that they went out to Burma for that purpose. They succeeded, and Harrap had the stones when he was captured by the dacoits. Are they in London? That is the question.'

'Do you suppose they are?' asked Malcolm Graeme.

'There is no telling,' Crane replied. 'I am satisfied, at all events, that no attempt has been made as yet to sell the rubies in England or on the Continent. A description of them was widely circulated, and if a single one of them had been disposed of, or offered for sale, the police would have known of it.'

'Will you investigate the matter on my behalf, Crane? I beg that you will. I have had the hope in mind since yesterday.'

'I should like to help you to regain what you have lost. It may be a very difficult thing, though, to — '

There was an interruption from Mary Graeme, who was in the room. She put a hand on the detective's shoulder

'Don't refuse, Mr. Crane,' she earnestly pleaded. 'Please don't! If the rubies are recovered it will mean so much to my father! And to me! When he came home in disgrace I was looking forward to going out to Burma with him in the autumn. I used to dream of his bungalow on the hillside smothered in flowers, and the picturesque life, and the beautiful tropical scenery! I wanted so badly to see it all! And now — and now — '

Her voice choked, and her eyes filled with tears. 'Please don't refuse!' she half-sobbed. 'Only you can help us!'

Crane gently patted the girl's hand.

'I had no intention of refusing my help,' he told her. 'I was merely going to point out that it may prove to be a very difficult task, if not an impossible one. Apart from my friendship with your father, and my desire to see him reinstated in his position, it would be a great satisfaction to me to bring to justice the guilty murderers. I have the time to spare, and I will do my best. As for the rubies, they may be somewhere in the wilds of Burma. Candidly, it is almost inconceivable that George Harrap was not robbed of them while he was a prisoner with the dacoits. Yet he may have brought them back, and if he did I shall probably be able to recover them.'

'Well, I shall hope for the best,' said Malcolm Graeme, 'and try to keep cheerful. To be living in respectable poverty in this cramped little house, in this big, noisy, crowded city — it is bitterly hard. But something seems to tell me I will be out in Burma again one of these days, at my old post.'

'You will be if I can accomplish it,' Crane replied. 'My first step will be to find Edgar Creed. That should not be difficult, and by having the man watched I shall doubtless get on the track of George Harrap, and John Burnley as well.

'I am glad you sent for me, Graeme,' he added, as he rose to go. 'What I have learned from you has thrown a new light on the affair of the ruby mines. I have the case well in hand, and I will let you know promptly if I make any progress.'

3

The Wounded Crook

For three days Lionel Crane and Pollard had been searching for Edgar Creed, and without the slightest success. They had not learned anything of him at the places he had been in the habit of frequenting. Men who were acquainted with him had declared, truthfully or falsely, that they had not seen him recently, and did not know where he was.

Though he was not wanted by the police, the crook had for some reason disappeared, and was keeping out of the way. And that was a very significant thing. It suggested, in view of what Malcolm Graeme had told the detective, that there might be a link between Edgar Creed and the stolen rubies.

Pollard came home at nine o'clock one night, tired and hungry, to find that Crane was still absent; and shortly

46

afterwards, as he was having his supper, he was startled by the sound of a pistol-shot somewhere in the neighbourhood.

A moment later he heard shouts, and the sudden throbbing of a car; and by the time he had dashed downstairs, and out of the house, a number of persons had gathered on the pavement about thirty yards or so from Crane's residence.

Pollard pushed into the crowd, and saw a constable whom he knew standing by the prostrate figure of a man who was bleeding from a wound in the chest, and was either dead or unconscious.

He was a well-dressed man, with a waxed moustache and a tuft of beard, and the shattered fragments of a monocle lay by his side. Pollard stared at him, and drew a quick breath.

'My word, this is a queer business!' he murmured. 'I wonder what it means?'

There was a stir of excitement in Welbeck Street. More people gathered, and another policeman came on the scene. He hastened away to send for an ambulance, and Pollard questioned the constable who had got there first.

'What do you know of this, Dean?' he asked.

'Not much,' was the reply. 'There must have been a quarrel. I passed two men who were talking at this spot, and I had got a little beyond Mr. Crane's house when I heard the report of a pistol, and looked back. I saw one of the men lying on the pavement, and saw the other jump into a taxi that was waiting close by. He was off like a streak, round the corner.'

'Did you hear anything the men said?'

'Not a word. They were talking in low tones.'

'Is this man dead, Dean?'

'No, he is breathing. I am afraid he is badly hurt, though. He is a stranger to me. Have you any idea who he is?'

Pollard nodded.

'Crane and I have been trying to find him for several days,' he whispered, putting a finger to his lips. 'He is a crook.'

'A crook, is he?' said the constable. 'He don't look like one. What's his name?'

'Edgar Creed.'

'Creed? Ah, that's the fellow who — '

48

'Keep it dark. Not a word. Crane doesn't want to have the man arrested. There isn't anything against him.'

More questions put by the young man elicited no further information from Constable Dean. He had not closely observed the man who had fired the shot. He could not identify him if he were to see him again. He had not noticed the cab until the assailant had jumped into it.

Pollard put a final question.

'Can you tell me in what direction the wounded man was going?' he inquired.

The constable could, as it happened.

'He was walking north, in the same direction as I was,' he stated. 'I had a glimpse of him in front of me before I got near, and I saw the other man catch up with him from behind and stop him. He couldn't have come in the taxi, for that was standing beyond him. It may not have been waiting for either of the men.'

The street was crowded, and more constables were on the scene, when at length the ambulance arrived. Edgar Creed, who was still unconscious, was carried off to Paddington Hospital. The spectators dispersed, and Pollard went home to wait for Crane.

★   ★   ★

Crane did not return until between eleven and twelve o'clock that night. As soon as he had heard Pollard's story he telephoned through to the Paddington Hospital, and was informed that Edgar Creed was not seriously injured, but that he was in a weak state after a slight operation, and he must be kept perfectly quiet for the present. The bullet, which had lodged in the muscles of the chest, had been extracted.

The next morning Crane telephoned again, and, having learned that the patient was much better, and could receive a visitor, he drove off to the hospital at once.

He had requested on the previous night that the wounded man should be put into a private room at his expense, and the house surgeon took him upstairs to a small and cheerful apartment and left him there.

Edgar Creed was in bed, propped amongst the pillows. Though he had not been told that the detective was coming to see him, he did not show any surprise, nor did he betray any uneasiness.

'It is very decent of you to pay me a visit, Mr. Crane,' he said brightly. 'So you have heard what happened last night?'

'Yes, from my partner,' Crane assented. 'It was a curious business, wasn't it?'

'Oh, no, not at all,' Edgar Creed calmly replied. 'A very simple affair.'

'You know who shot you, of course?'

'I do not, sir. I was walking up Welbeck Street, on my way to call on a friend, when I was stopped by a strange man. He demanded money. I refused to give him any, and he pulled out a pistol and fired. That is all I can remember.'

Crane had quite expected to hear some such a tale, and he was the more convinced, from the absurdity of it, that the crook had good reasons for wishing to conceal the truth. It was doubtful, he felt, if he would succeed in getting any information. He was not discouraged, however.

'It is impossible for me to believe your story,' he said. 'It was no footpad who shot you. The man talked to you for some little time before he fired, and he afterwards escaped in a taxi that was waiting for him nearby.'

'That may be,' Edgar Creed answered. 'I did not see any cab in the vicinity. Why are you so interested in this trivial matter?'

'Because I have certain suspicions,' Crane declared.

The crook shrugged his shoulders.

'You are deceiving yourself,' he said. 'I cannot imagine what you can suspect me of. The police have nothing whatever against me.'

'I don't deny that. I have been trying to find you, though, for the last three days.'

'Go on, sir. What have you up your sleeve?'

'Not long ago, Creed, you were seen in Piccadilly with George Harrap.'

'Quite right. He is an old friend of mine.'

'And so is John Burnley, I dare say. Is

he in London, too?'

'I can't tell you. I haven't seen anything of him.'

'Some few months ago,' Crane resumed, 'a crime was committed at the ruby mines of Mogok, in Upper Burma. A clerk was cruelly murdered, and a parcel of rubies, worth two hundred thousand pounds, was stolen from the safe. John Burnley and George Harrap were in Burma at the time, in camp near the mines, and suspicion fell on them.'

For just an instant Edgar Creed changed colour.

'I have heard the story,' he said. 'It was in the newspapers, and I had a fuller account from Harrap. Both men were innocent. They were wrongly suspected.'

'Do you think so?'

'I am certain of it, Mr. Crane.'

'There was little or no evidence against them, I will admit. On the night of the robbery they were attacked in the jungle by a band of dacoits. John Burnley got away and came to my camp. He was arrested, and was subsequently released. George Harrap was carried off a prisoner, and by some means he contrived to escape.'

'Yes, I know all about that. It does not interest me in the least.'

Crane paused for a moment.

'Did George Harrap bring the rubies back to England with him?' he sharply rapped out. 'Did he?'

Edgar Creed was too much on his guard to be caught in the trap.

'It is a stupid question to put to me,' he quietly replied. 'As I have already told you, to the best of my belief Harrap and Burnley were innocent. If they were not, be assured they have not taken me into their confidence since they returned.'

'They? You said you had not seen anything of Burnley.'

'That is true. I was referring to Harrap.'

'No, you have seen them both. I am sure of it.'

Edgar Creed did not answer. He merely shrugged his shoulders again. Crane hesitated. Should he show all his cards or not? If he were to do so, he reflected, he might induce the crook to open his lips.

'I put it to you,' he went on, 'that when

you were shot last night you were on the way to see me?'

Edgar Creed appeared to be genuinely surprised.

'It is absurd!' he exclaimed. 'What could I have wanted to see you about?'

'To give me information about the stolen rubies,' said Crane. 'To claim the large reward that has been offered for their recovery.'

'You are very far wrong, sir. I have not the slightest knowledge of the rubies.'

'Furthermore, Creed, I put it to you that it was either Burnley or Harrap who shot you?'

'Certainly not. What motive could either of the men have had for wishing to murder me?'

'I can suggest a plausible one. They had refused to comply with some demand of yours, and you had threatened to denounce them to me. That is what I believe.'

'Denounce them for what?'

'The theft of the rubies, Creed.'

'My dear Mr. Crane, how many times must I tell you that to the best of my knowledge those men had nothing to do with the robbery in Burma. And if they had it would be no business of mine.'

'If you knew they had it would be like you to try to get a share of the spoils. You have played that game before.'

'And I would play it again if I had the chance. I haven't, though. You are letting your imagination run away with you.'

Crane was chagrined by his failure. The crook, seeing through the motive for the visit, had coolly foiled every attempt to draw him out. He had told lie after lie.

The circumstances under which he had been shot, the locality, his refusal to tell who had tried to kill him — these things clearly indicated that he had been on his way to the detective's residence on the previous night.

And he had been going there for only one purpose. Why would he not disclose that purpose now? What had brought about this change of mind? Had he concluded to have another try at the game he had unsuccessfully played?

Crane thought so.

'Can't you see that it would be to your

advantage to be frank with me?' he urged. 'When thieves rob thieves they usually come to grief. You have had one warning. Don't risk your life again. Help me to recover the rubies, and the reward will be yours.'

Edgar Creed yawned, and turned over to the wall.

'I am tired and sleepy,' he said, in a languid tone. 'I can't talk any more, Mr. Crane. You can call another time if you like.'

Crane was utterly baffled. He went downstairs, and when he had learned from the house surgeon that the crook would probably be discharged in three or four days, he left the hospital and drove home. And while he was at luncheon he told Pollard of his fruitless efforts to get at the truth.

'I was not in the least deceived,' he continued. 'It is all as plain as a pikestaff. Knowing that John Burnley and George Harrap were guilty of the robbery and murder at the mines of Mogok, Edgar Creed tried to blackmail them. They refused to pay, and he threatened to come

57

to me. They set a watch on him, and he was shot by one of the men last night as he was about to carry out his threat.

'But did he know that the rubies were in their possession, that Harrap had brought them back from Burma with him? I can't be sure. Perhaps he attempted to blackmail them merely because he knew of the crime they had committed, and he meant to denounce them to me out of revenge, not with any expectation of receiving the reward for the recovery of the jewels. Be that as it may, he has changed his mind since he was shot. We will have to wait until he leaves the hospital, and then we will keep him under surveillance.'

'And won't you do anything in the meantime?' asked Pollard. 'What of Harrap and Burnley? We ought to find them.'

Crane nodded absently, and was silent for a little while.

'I have been thinking,' he said. 'Harrap and Burnley have read the morning papers, of course. They are aware by now that Creed has not made any statement about them, and that he intends to screen them. But they must be in fear of his revenge. What will they do? Try to leave the country? Probably they will, and if the rubies are in their possession they will be anxious to get rid of them as soon as they can. They will attempt to dispose of them. And how? It is to be presumed that — '

He paused abruptly. 'You remember Isador Cohen?' he added.

'Of Queen Street, Seven Dials?' said Pollard.

'That is the man,' Crane replied. 'He is the most daring fence in London, and at the present time the only one who would not hesitate to buy stolen property which had been described in the papers. If Harrap and Burnley are professional crooks — and doubtless they are, from their association with Edgar Creed — they must know of Isador Cohen. And if so they will almost certainly go to him with the rubies.'

'Provided they have them, Li.'

'I strongly believe they have. In all likelihood it was a share of the rubies Creed demanded of the men, not hush money.'

Crane rose as he spoke.

'I shall see Isador Cohen without delay,' he declared. 'He will be like wax in my hands. With his help I will set a neat little trap, and those two crooks may walk into it before Edgar Creed is out of the hospital.'

4

A Signal From the Street

On the night of the following day, towards nine o'clock, a tall man with a fair moustache and a bronzed complexion crossed Seven Dials and turned into Queen Street.

He stopped near the farther end of that thoroughfare, threw a furtive glance behind him, and entered a pawnbroking establishment. Seeing no one there, he walked by the counter to a small window that had a shelf in front of it, and was set in a glass partition.

He stood there for a few seconds, and then the pawnbroker came forward from an office at the back of the premises, and peered through the window. He was an elderly, stoop-shouldered man, clad in a shabby velvet jacket; a sinister-looking man with wrinkled features, a grey beard and moustache, and thick, greasy hair.

61

'Well Isador, how are things going?' asked the visitor.

Isador Cohen scrutinised him closely.

'I am afraid I can't remember you,' he gruffly replied.

'You've not forgotten John Burnley, have you?'

'John Burnley? Ah, I recognise you now! It is a long time since I've seen you.'

'Yes, there haven't been any dealings between us for a couple of years. I was in America for a while, and recently I have been in the Far East.'

'I knew that. There was a lot in the papers about you and George Harrap. You got into trouble out in Burma.'

'That's right,' said John Burnley. 'And we got out of it.'

'You hadn't anything to do with the robbery and murder at the ruby mines — eh?' inquired the pawnbroker;

'Hadn't we? Don't be too sure. I have something to show you. But tell me first if the police have been to see you.'

'No, I've not had a visit from them.'

'Or from Lionel Crane?'

'He's not been here either.'

John Burnley nodded. He went to the door and locked it, and returned to the window. Then he took from his pocket an envelope, and shook from it, on to the shelf, a red stone that was as big as a filbert, and glowed and sparkled as if there was a flame inside of it.

'What do you think of that?' he said. 'Isn't it a beauty?'

Isador Cohen stared in amazement. 'A — a pigeon-blood ruby!' he gasped. 'I never saw one like it before!'

'You bet you didn't, Isador. It's a monster. Of the purest water and colour.'

'So you and Harrap really did — '

'Yes, we got away with the swag. Harrap had the stones, fifty of them, when he was caught by the dacoits. They didn't find them on him, though.'

'Where are the rest, Burnley? Have you got them with you?'

'No fear. They are safely hidden. And now what are you going to give me for this?'

The pawnbroker shook his head.

'There is nothing doing,' he declared. 'It would be too dangerous.'

'Dangerous?' John Bumley repeated. 'For you, who know all the tricks of the game. Why?'

'I couldn't dispose of it. I should be afraid to try. The rubies have been described in all the newspapers in England and abroad.'

'That doesn't matter. The affair has been almost forgotten by now.'

Isador Cohen shook his head again.

'It's no use in talking about it,' he said.

'But I've got to have money, and quick at that,' John Burnley urged. 'I simply must. Come, don't be windy. Let us strike a bargain. There's a man in London who has his knife into us, Harrap and me, because of an old grudge, and we want to cross to the Continent as soon as we can. The trouble is we're both almost stony-broke.'

'I can't help that. I tell you again it would be too dangerous for me to buy this stone. What if the police were to find it in my possession?'

'There isn't any fear of that, Isador. It is believed that the dacoits stole the rubies.'

'I'm not taking any chances. I daren't.'

John Burnley shrugged his shoulders. He picked up the ruby from the shelf, slipped it into the envelope, and replaced it in his pocket.

'Well, if you won't, you won't,' he said. 'Never mind. I'll find another market for it, and inside of an hour.'

The pawnbroker hesitated.

'Wait a moment,' he bade. 'Perhaps I'll think better of it. It depends on the price. How much do you want?'

'I'll let it go dirt cheap, as I need the money so badly. Say two thousand pounds.'

'Two thousand! Nothing like it, Burnley!'

'But the ruby is worth four thousand.'

'It may be, in the ordinary market. Not to me.'

'What will you give? Name your figure.'

'Six hundred pounds.'

'That's ridiculous, Isador. Don't try to take a mean advantage of me.'

'I am thinking of the risk I should be running. Where could I safely dispose of such a large and valuable stone?'

'You wouldn't have any difficulty,' said John Burnley. 'Make it a thousand, at the least.'

'No, six hundred,' Isador Cohen replied. 'I can't go above that. Take it or leave it.'

John Burnley was silent for a moment.

'Very well, then,' he sullenly assented. 'I'll have to take six hundred, you old Shylock. It's a case of necessity. Hand over the money, and I'll be off.'

'I can't pay you now. It is impossible. I banked just before three o'clock this afternoon.'

'Confound the luck! How long will I have to wait?'

'Until tomorrow, Burnley. Come back at eleven o'clock in the morning, and the money will be ready for you.'

'Isn't there enough in your safe?'

'No, I never keep more than a few pounds there for any length of time. The safe was robbed once, and since then — '

As the pawnbroker spoke a shrill whistle was heard. It was twice repeated. John Burnley gave a quick start, and turned pale.

'I believe you've set a trap for me, curse you!' he snarled.

A suspicion flashed to his mind. He gazed closely at the old man, and then, reaching for him through the window, he grasped his beard and moustache, and plucked them from his face.

'By heavens, Crane!' he cried. 'Lionel Crane!'

Whipping round, he rushed to the door, unlocked it and flung it open, and darted outside. He had already disappeared when Crane got to the street. He looked in all directions, and, seeing no running figure in sight, he returned to the shop. The real Isador Cohen had come from his office at the rear of the premises.

'Ah, that was good!' he chuckled, rubbing his hands together. 'Very good, sir! I enjoyed it. You played the part perfectly. The fellow had not a suspicion until he — '

'Until he heard that whistle,' Crane interrupted.

'You think it was a signal of danger, sir?'

'No doubt it was, Cohen. There must have been somebody keeping watch outside. George Harrap, I suppose.'

'It is a pity. I am afraid you have missed an opportunity, Mr. Crane.'

'I fear so. On the whole, however, my little ruse has been a success.'

Pollard, who had been posted in the vicinity, now came in, panting for breath.

'I've lost the rascal,' he said. 'What went wrong, Li? Did he tumble to the game?'

Crane nodded, and briefly related what had occurred.

'I dare say you noticed George Harrap lurking about,' he resumed.

'I saw a man standing over the way,' Pollard replied. 'It didn't strike me that it might be Harrap until he whistled. I guessed then he had seen me standing on the pavement opposite to him, and suspected who I was. When John Burnley came dashing out, I let him go by, and gave chase. He ran to the Seven Dials, where he was joined by Harrap. The two of them got into a taxi, and there wasn't another one near, so I had to come back.

It is hard luck, isn't it?'

'It might have been worse.'

'It is bad enough, Li. The men have had a bad fright. They will be on their guard after this, and will lie low.'

'We will get them in the end, though.'

Crane told Pollard of his conversation with the crook. He was not greatly disappointed. He had not intended to arrest John Burnley after he learned that he had not all the rubies with him. He had meant to let Pollard shadow him, and thus find out where he lived.

That purpose had been frustrated, but he was compensated for his failure by the information he had gleaned. The doubtful point — the point on which everything depended — had been definitely settled.

'We know now, Harry,' he said, 'that the stolen rubies were brought back from Burma, and that they are in the possession of Burnley and Harrap. We also know that the men have little or no money, and, that being the case, they will have to stay in London for the present, instead of crossing to the Continent.'

'Perhaps they will make another attempt to sell one of the rubies,' Pollard answered.

'No, they wouldn't risk that. They would be afraid. On second thoughts, though, they may raise money somewhere, and try to escape abroad with the rubies.'

'You ought to take steps to prevent them from getting away, Li.'

'I intend to, Harry. And without delay.'

Crane removed his wig, and changed the jacket he had borrowed from the pawnbroker for his own coat; and a few moments later he and Pollard were driving to Scotland Yard in a taxi.

They had an interview with Inspector Pidgeon, who had previously been informed of the case the detective was working on; and when they left the Yard, and went home, it was with the assurance that a watch would be set for the two crooks at the big railway stations of London, and at the Channel ports as well.

Crane was satisfied with what progress he had so far made, and the next morning he sent to Hammersmith a telegram that gladdened the hearts of Malcolm Graeme and his daughter. It ran as follows.

'Have learned to a certainty that the stolen rubies are in the possession of Burnley and Harrap. Every hope of recovery.

— Crane.'

5

The House in Langham Street

There had been no news, as yet, of the two crooks when, just after darkness had fallen one evening, Edgar Creed was discharged from the Paddington Hospital.

There was burning rage in his heart. He craved for revenge as a man suffering from thirst craves for water. Vengeance he would have, and more than that, unless his intentions should be frustrated by Lionel Crane. He took it for granted, naturally, that the detective would try to keep him under surveillance, and that he had been notified of the hour at which he would be discharged.

So he was very much on his guard after he left the institution. At frequent intervals, as he walked slowly along Praed Street, he stopped to look behind him. On reaching the Edgware Road, he went into a public house, and as he stood at the bar drinking he scanned the passers-by, and took a survey of the opposite side of the street as well.

So far he had seen nothing to confirm his suspicions. Having finished his drink, he entered a 'bus, and frequently glanced back all the way to the Marble Arch. Now, certain that no one had followed him in a cab, he concluded there was no ground for his apprehensions.

'It might have occurred to me,' he reflected, 'that Crane would not have considered it worth his while to have me shadowed. I dare say he has been trying to find Burnley and Harrap, and without any success. They must be lying low, curse them!'

Shrewd though Edgar Creed had been, however, he had not been clever enough for Lionel Crane's young assistant. Seated on top of the 'bus was a shabbily-dressed youth, and that youth was no other than Pollard. Favoured by the darkness, and the crowded pavements, he had followed the crook from the hospital without being detected.

Edgar Creed rode only as far as Oxford

Circus. He left the 'bus there, and struck up Great Portland Street; turned into Langham Street, and stopped in front of a dwelling that had an apartment card displayed in a window.

It was obvious that he lived here. He opened the door with a latchkey and went in; and when he reappeared a quarter of an hour later he was disguised by a false beard and a pair of spectacles. But he was wearing the same clothes, and Pollard, not for an instant deceived, took up the chase again.

Edgar Creed was no longer suspicious. Not once did he look back. At a brisk pace he walked down Regent Street to Piccadilly Circus, round by the Haymarket, and thence to Orange Street, where he paused in front of a house that was to the east of Whitcomb Street. He rang the bell, and the door was opened by an elderly woman.

'I am looking for an apartment, madam,' said Edgar Creed. 'Some months ago I called here to see a friend who had a room at the back, on the second floor. The door of the room opposite happened to be open, and I saw inside. It was a large room, comfortably furnished, and I would like to have it if it is vacant.'

The woman shook her head.

'You are a few hours too late, sir,' she replied. 'The two gentlemen who had the room gave it up last Monday, and it was vacant until this morning, when I let it to somebody else.'

'I am very sorry to hear that. By the way, I think I knew the gentlemen who had the room before. Can you tell me where they have gone?'

'No, sir, I haven't any idea. As for your wanting a room, there is a vacant one on the top floor. Perhaps it would suit you.'

'No, thank you, madam. I will try elsewhere. Good evening!'

Edgar Creed had been in the house on several occasions, and by a clever stratagem, without mentioning any names, he had learned from the landlady what he wished to know.

It was to see John Burnley and George Harrap that he had called here before, and, as he had anticipated, they were gone. They had departed on the previous

Monday, and on the night of that day he, Creed, had been shot in Welbeck Street. He was in a furious temper.

'The sneaking, yellow curs!' he said to himself, as he walked towards Whitcomb Street. 'Where the deuce am I to look for them? I'll find them sooner or later, though, and I'll strip them of every blamed ruby! I'll be even with them!'

Pollard, lurking in the background, had not been able to hear any of the conversation with the woman. He continued to shadow Edgar Creed, who crossed Coventry Street, and went north into the Soho quarter, where he entered the Café Spartos in Bateman Street.

He did not go through to the room at the rear. He seated himself at a table in a corner of the front room, and ordered a small bottle of wine; and presently, catching the proprietor's eye, he beckoned to him. The Greek, as big a rogue as there was in London, came over to him.

'You wish to speak to me?' he inquired.

Edgar Creed nodded.

'That's right,' he answered.

'I don't think I know you, sir.'

'Oh, yes, you do, Spartos. Look closely.'

Marc Spartos stared for a moment, and then sat down.

'Why are you disguised, Creed?' he said in a whisper.

'For a good reason,' Edgar Creed replied, in a low tone. 'You know what happened to me, I suppose.'

'I read it in the papers. Somebody shot you in Welbeck Street on Monday night. Have you any idea who it was?'

'Yes. It was George Harrap.'

'How was that? He had a grudge against you?'

'He thought he had; and now I have a grudge against him, and John Burnley, too. I want to find them badly.'

'Aren't they still in Orange Street?' asked the Greek.

'No, they left there on Monday,' said Edgar Creed, with an oath. 'They have disappeared, and they will keep out of my way if they can. You haven't seen anything of them, I dare say?'

'I haven't seen Burnley all the week, but Harrap was in here last evening.'

'Ah, was he?'

'Yes; he sat in the outer room for a while. He was alone, and disguised. He had a false beard and moustache.'

'Are you sure it was Harrap?'

'I am positive of it, Creed. I knew him by the queer ring he wears. I have often noticed it. That gave him away, and so did his voice. I heard him talking to the waiter.'

'You didn't let him know you had recognised him, did you?'

'No, I didn't speak to him. I thought I had better not.'

'The dirty hound!' muttered Edgar Creed, a savage glitter in his eyes. 'Wait till I get hold of him! He ventured here because he is fond of that old wine of yours, and it is not to be had anywhere else.'

'That's what he drank last night,' replied Marc Spartos. 'The same vintage.'

'He may come in again. If he does, will you have somebody follow him when he leaves, and learn where he is living?'

'I'll see to that, Creed. You can depend on me.'

'Very well. It will be to your advantage.

I will give you five pounds for the information.'

'And Burnley? If he should come in?'

'Have him followed, of course.'

The Greek returned to his place at the bar, throwing a careless glance at a youth who was seated at a table nearby. It was Pollard who sat there, and, having uncommonly sharp ears, he had heard almost every word of the conversation.

In about half an hour Edgar Creed left the café, and, still shadowed by the young man, he went on foot to Langham Street, and entered the house where he lodged.

Pollard's work was finished for the night. Elated by his success, he picked up a taxi and drove home, and told the whole story to Lionel Crane, who warmly praised him for his cleverness.

'The Café Spartos!' he continued. 'A villainous den! I know all about Marc Spartos, the proprietor. The information you got is of the greatest value. It probably won't be long until we have the rubies, Harry.'

'I should think so, Li,' said Pollard.

'Yes, it looks as if the end of the case is

in sight,' Crane replied. 'There is good reason to believe so. We know where Creed is living, and one or the other of us will keep a close eye on him. If Burnley and Harrap are in London — and I don't doubt it — in all likelihood Marc Spartos will succeed in finding out where they are hiding. He will tell Edgar Creed, and by shadowing Edgar Creed we shall have an opportunity of arresting the two crooks. And the rubies will be found in their possession.'

6

The Tragedy of the Hotel Dijon

At the hour of ten at night, two days after he was discharged from the hospital, Edgar Creed came out of his lodgings in Langham Street, and strolled leisurely to Oxford Circus. He was again disguised by spectacles and a false beard, and he had brought with him, in case of need, a loaded automatic pistol.

He entered the Tube station in Oxford Street, and stepped into a telephone booth, rang up the Exchange, and was put through to the Café Spartos. The familiar voice of Marc Spartos called:

'Who is it?'

'Creed is speaking,' the crook answered. 'Have you any news for me yet?'

'Yes, there is good news,' said the Greek. 'George Harrap has been here this evening, disguised as he was before.'

'He isn't there now?'

'No, he has gone.'

'You had him followed, I hope?'

'I saw to that, Creed. When Harrap left, an hour ago, I sent the waiter Alphonse after him. Alphonse returned shortly afterwards, and told me Harrap had gone to the Hotel Dijon, in Long Acre.'

'Do you suppose he lives there?'

'I should think so. Alphonse said he walked straight along the hall and up the stairs.'

'Thanks very much, Spartos. I will fix things with you later. I may be in some time tonight. Goodbye!'

Edgar Creed rang off, and left the booth whistling under his breath, an evil smile on his face, and a gleam of satisfaction in his eyes. Revenge was almost in his grasp, he felt — so profitable a revenge that he would be able to lead a life of ease and luxury in his beloved capitals of Europe.

Uncertain as to just what steps he should take to achieve his purpose, he got into a taxi, and was driven to Cranbourn Street. From there he walked along Long Acre, and stopped on the pavement at a dark spot that was directly opposite to the Hotel Dijon.

'Burnley is living here, too, of course,' he murmured. 'The cunning of the rogues! They knew I wouldn't dream of finding them anywhere so near to Orange Street.'

The Hotel Dijon was a tall, narrow dwelling of four stories, shabby in appearance. It was a French hotel, and was in every respect similar to the cheap residential hotels that abound in Paris.

The entrance was wide open, and one could see within. A short stretch of hall, furnished with a rattan couch and two chairs, led to the staircase; and to the right of the hall was a cosy apartment, which the proprietor used as a living room and as a bureau.

Edgar Creed had been standing on the pavement for some minutes, still in a state of indecision, when a man came down the stairs, and passed quickly out to the street. A cap was pulled low on his brow, and the collar of his coat was muffled about his chin.

He bore to the left, and walked away at a rapid pace. A startling suspicion now flashed to Edgar Creed's mind. He whipped across the road, and took chase after the man, who looked over his shoulder, and at once took to his heels, running like a deer.

Edgar Creed chased him for a short distance, and, having lost sight of him in a dark thoroughfare off Long Acre, he abandoned the pursuit; hastened to the Hotel Dijon, and entered. He stopped short in the hall, and stared at a man who was sitting on the couch

'Ah, Mr. Crane!' he said, in a tone of forced calmness.

Crane nodded.

'Hello, Creed!' he replied.

'What are you doing here, sir?'

'My business is the same as yours, perhaps.'

'I understand. You have been shadowing me tonight.'

'You are not far wrong. Isn't it natural that I should take an interest in your movements?'

There was a brief silence. From the

time Edgar Creed had left his lodgings in Langham Street he had been followed by Crane, who, while watching in Long Acre, had seen the man who had hurried from the hotel, had seen Creed give chase to him, and had seen him turn back. He would have given chase himself had he not been too far off.

Edgar Creed was quite cool.

'I should very much like to know,' he remarked, 'how you got on my track?'

'That is of no importance,' Crane answered. 'I prefer to talk of other matters. You were aware, of course, that your friends Burnley and Harrap have been living in the Hotel Dijon.'

'I was not aware of anything of the sort.'

'Who was the man you pursued a little while ago?'

'I have no idea, Mr. Crane.'

'Indeed? Why did you chase him?'

'Because his movements were suspicious. That was the reason.'

'I thought the same, Creed. Apparently there is nothing wrong here, though. It would seem not.'

'I am not so sure about that.'

Crane did not reply. He was puzzled and uneasy. All was quiet. The bureau was deserted. Jacques Laparde, the proprietor, was not there.

'Let us go above,' said Edgar Creed. 'I am afraid that — '

'Listen!' Crane interrupted.

Somebody was coming down the stairs, descending with heavy, floundering steps. He came on and on, and at length there appeared a little, elderly Frenchman with a grey moustache, and grey hair that bristled straight up from his head. It was Jacques Laparde. He was ghastly white, and his eyes were staring wildly. He was acquainted with the detective.

'Mr. Crane!' he gasped. 'Murder! I fear so! Fetch the police!'

'What has happened?' asked Crane.

'I — I don't know yet!' stammered the proprietor. 'I have been up in my bedroom, which is at the top of the house, and at the back! I was there for some time, searching for something I could not find! And as I was coming down I noticed blood trickling from

86

beneath the door of the front room on the second floor.'

'Who occupies that room?'

'A gentleman of the name of Baird!'

'You didn't look in?'

'No, sir, I — I was too frightened!'

Jacques Laparde and Crane started up the stairs, and Edgar Creed followed them.

They found the door of the front room on the second floor unlocked. The light was burning inside, and it revealed a terrible sight.

In a huddled attitude on the floor was the dead body of a man with a fair moustache and a sunburnt complexion, and near him lay a bloodstained poker. It was obvious, from the state of the room, that there had been a fearful struggle.

The dead man had been killed with brutal ferocity — killed by at least half a dozen smashing blows that had crushed and splintered his skull. His clothes were drenched in blood, and there were purple marks on his throat. Blood was sprinkled everywhere — on the carpet, on chairs, on a table, on a couch. And there were red fingerprints on the walls.

'This is John Burnley!' declared Crane, when he had thrown a sweeping glance around him.

Edgar Creed's face was a study of mingled emotions.

'Yes, it is Burnley,' he assented, in a rasping voice.

Jacques Laparde was like one daft, wringing his hands, moaning and gibbering. As for Crane, he felt as if the earth had caved under his feet. His hopes had been shattered. He knew that the rubies were gone. All was clear to him.

'Didn't you hear any cries for help, any sounds of a struggle?' he asked of the proprietor.

'No, sir, I didn't hear anything,' Jacques Laparde tremulously replied.

'I can account for that,' said Crane. 'It was almost a silent struggle. The murderer had his victim tightly by the throat while he floundered about the room with him, raining blows on his head. Something started a quarrel between the two men, and there was a mad, desperate fight. They doubtless had a dispute over the — '

He broke off abruptly.

'You know as well as I do, Creed,' he said, 'that George Harrap is the murderer.'

'It couldn't have been anybody else,' Edgar Creed answered.

'You learned from Marc Spartos, on the telephone,' Crane continued, 'that John Burnley was staying at the Hotel Dijon. Did he also find out for you where Harrap was living?'

'He did not, sir. As a matter of fact, the information he got for me was misleading. I was under the impression that both of the men were at the hotel, for the Greek had Harrap shadowed here from the Café Spartos. I can't help you to find him. I would if I could.'

'I doubt that. I know the game you have been playing.'

Edgar Creed shrugged his shoulders, wondering how much knowledge the detective had. While he spoke he had been looking about him, and now he sauntered carelessly towards the window, stopped, and took a cigarette from his pocket.

Crane, his suspicions suddenly aroused, stepped over to him, and pushed him aside. And then, stooping, he picked up from the floor a flaming red jewel.

'A clever trick!' he said sharply. 'It didn't work, though.'

Creed bit his lip.

'I didn't notice the stone,' he declared. 'It is one of the rubies from the Burmese mines.'

'You did notice it. You deliberately put your foot on it. You would have stolen it if you had got the chance.'

'That is not true, sir. But have it your own way. I won't argue. I am intruding here, so I had better go.'

'Not yet. You will stay where you are for the present. I am going to send for the police.'

'You don't intend to have me arrested, of course.'

'Arrested? What for, Creed? I know of no charge that could be brought against you.'

Crane did not leave at once. He had

already felt in the dead man's pockets, and it was not until he had thoroughly searched the room, and was satisfied that the rubies were not here, that he went downstairs.

Having locked the front door, and taken the key from the lock, he entered the bureau. He telephoned to Inspector Pidgeon at Scotland Yard, and told him to come to the Hotel Dijon without delay; and afterwards he got through to Pollard, and gave him certain instructions.

'Be as quick as you can, Harry,' he bade, as he rang off.

He unlocked and opened the front door again, and returned to the scene of the tragedy. Edgar Creed was sitting in a chair, with moody, sullen eyes, gazing at the corpse.

'I want all the information you can give me,' Crane said to the proprietor, who had recovered from the shock. 'How long has this man Burnley been at the hotel?'

'Only for a few days,' Jacques Laparde replied. 'He came last Monday, and gave the name of Baird.'

'He came alone?'

'He was alone, sir.'

'He has had a visitor?'

'Yes, a dark man with a beard and moustache called to see him several times.'

'You have seen that man tonight?'

'I did, Mr. Crane. He passed along the hall, and ascended the stairs, while I was in the bureau. And afterwards, when I went up to my bedroom, I heard him talking to Mr. Baird in this room.'

'Did you hear what they said, Laparde?'

'No, they were talking very low, in whispers.'

'Has your lodger been out often?' Crane resumed.

'He hasn't been out since he came,' said the proprietor. 'I thought it very queer. He has had his meals in the hotel.'

'He paid for them?'

'He hasn't paid a penny. He told me he was getting a large remittance shortly, and I let him have credit.'

'Nobody has been to see him except the man who was here tonight?'

'There has been no one else, Mr. Crane.'

The statements made by Jacques

Laparde established two facts that were of importance. Since the two crooks were about at the end of their resources — had one had money he would have shared with the other — it was clear that none of the stolen rubies had as yet been disposed of. And, furthermore, it was certain that George Harrap was the murderer.

The two men had been living in different places, hiding from the vengeance of the man whose life they had attempted. The rubies, it was to be presumed, had been entrusted to John Burnley for safe keeping. Harrap had come tonight from the Café Spartos to the Hotel Dijon. He had killed Burnley, and he subsequently fled with the stones.

Had there been a dispute over them to start with? Had Harrap struck those terrible blows in hot blood, in blind rage? Or had he purposely, deliberately, murdered Burnley that he might have all the rubies himself? The latter was the more probable.

Crane turned to Edgar Creed. 'We have both been foiled tonight, you rascal,' he said coldly.

'I have been foiled?' Creed replied. 'What do you mean?'

'Don't pretend to misunderstand me. From the first it was your intention to rob your friends of the rubies. That is why you have been trying to find them.'

'Not at all, Mr. Crane. My object in trying to find George Harrap was to have him arrested for shooting me on Monday night.'

'Ah, you admit now that you knew who shot you!'

'Yes, it was Harrap.'

'Well, you needn't say any more. As I told you before, I know the game you have been playing, and I warn you now to drop it. If you persist in your efforts to find George Harrap, and cross my path again, it will go very hard with you. Bear that in mind.'

At a word from the detective, Jacques Laparde withdrew, and went down to the bureau. Edgar Creed did not stir. He sat still, smoking cigarette after cigarette, while Crane paced the floor, chaffing under his defeat. It was a bitter disappointment to him.

Presently a cab was heard to stop in the street, and a few moments later Inspector Pidgeon came upstairs and went into the room, accompanied by two of his men.

'Good heavens, Crane, what a brutal murder!' he cried in horror, as he glanced about him. 'This is one of the crooks you have been searching for, I suppose?'

'It is John Burnley,' Crane answered.

'And the murderer?'

'His friend and accomplice, Harrap. He has carried off the rubies. They were the motive for the crime.'

'And this man here?' asked the inspector. 'Had he anything to do with the — ' He paused abruptly. 'Hello, I believe it is Edgar Creed!' he exclaimed in surprise.

'Quite right,' Crane assented. 'I have been shadowing him tonight, and he led me to the Hotel Dijon. That was before the murder was discovered.'

'And you have detained Creed?'

'No, there isn't anything against him. He is at liberty to go. I have given him a warning, and he will be wise to heed it.'

Edgar Creed rose from his chair.

'Goodnight, Inspector,' he said, as he strolled to the door. 'Goodnight, Mr. Crane. You have my address, if you should wish to see me at any time.'

He passed jauntily out of the room, screwing a monocle into his eye; and he had no more than got to the bottom of the stairs when Crane stepped to the window, opened it, and gazed beneath him. He quietly shut the window, and turned away.

'It is all right,' he said. 'I telephoned to Pollard after I rang you up, and he is standing on the other side of the street. He saw me and waved his hand. I hope Creed won't discover he is being shadowed. It is not likely he will. Harry knows his business.'

He gave Inspector Pidgeon a full account of the events of the night, and made clear to him the cunning part Edgar Creed had been playing in the affair.

'We were both foiled, as I told him,' he went on. 'It was a blow to me. I was confident the rubies would soon be recovered.'

'You will have to be patient,' replied the

inspector. 'It won't be an easy task to find the man Harrap.'

'It will be a most difficult one. Only so the fellow doesn't contrive to escape abroad. The watch at the railway stations and at the Channel ports must be continued.'

'They will be. I will see to that. By the way, Crane, I don't believe Harrap and Burnley are the real names of those men. I have never heard of them.'

'I haven't, either. I haven't a doubt that they are professional crooks in assumed names. If so it will not be difficult to find out who they really are.'

'How can we?'

'Look at the wall,' bade Crane. 'Do you see the fingerprints? They are Harrap's.'

'Or Burnley's,' said Inspector Pidgeon.

'No, there isn't a trace of blood on his fingers. The prints were made by Harrap.'

'That's right. They must be photographed. I will send one of my men to Scotland Yard for a camera.'

'You needn't trouble,' said Crane. 'I am going home now to fetch my camera. I will take a photograph of the fingerprints on the wall, and also an impression of John Burnley's fingers. Very likely there is a duplicate of them at the Yard.'

He shook his head gravely as he spoke. 'One could almost believe there is a curse on the stolen rubies,' he added. 'They have cost two lives already, and they may be the cause of more bloodshed before they are recovered.'

'If they ever are,' said the inspector.

Crane's eyes narrowed. 'They will be,' he declared. 'I shall get them in the end.'

He spoke with confidence, and he was confident. He would surmount every obstacle, let nothing deter him. He knew just what he was up against, and there was in his heart the conviction that he would ultimately succeed.

But as he was driving from Long Acre to Welbeck Street in a cab, thinking of the tragic development in the case, he had a premonition, as it were, that the prediction he had made to Inspector Pidgeon would be fulfilled — that not until the fatal rubies had cost more lives would Malcolm Graeme return to his post in Burma.

7

What the Fingerprint Records at Scotland Yard Established

It could readily have been believed, from Edgar Creed's actions after he left the Hotel Dijon, that he had not the slightest expectation of being shadowed, and that it would not be worth his while to take precautions.

Warily dogged by Pollard, who had lost no time in obeying the instructions telephoned to him by Crane, the crook strolled from Long Acre to Leicester Square, not once looking behind him.

He went into the Tube station, where he held a short conversation with somebody in one of the telephone booths; and when he came out he went on to Piccadilly Circus and from there to Glasshouse Street, stopped at the Bodega for a drink, and then, walked slowly up Regent Street, mingling with the people who were flocking homeward from restaurants and theatres.

He might easily have eluded his pursuer by getting into a taxi at a moment when there was only one to be had, but he did not take advantage of his frequent opportunities. Was he really unsuspicious, or had he some cunning purpose in mind?

Be which it may, he sauntered carelessly on to Oxford Circus, with never a backward glance, and crossed over to Great Portland Street, followed that thoroughfare, turned into Langham Street, and paused in front of Number 94, where he lived. He lit a cigarette, opened the door with his latchkey, and entered the house.

Pollard stood close by the wall to one side so that he could not be seen from any window above, and considered the situation. He had not been hoodwinked by the ease with which he had tracked the crook to his lodgings. It had been overdone.

Edgar Creed was no fool. Knowing that Lionel Crane had gone down to the bureau to use the telephone, he must have taken it for granted that some person would be watching for him when he left the Hotel Dijon. On the assumption that he believed he had been shadowed, therefore, what were his intentions?

Would he stay where he was until tomorrow, and then try to slip off unobserved? Or would he make an attempt tonight? If so, how? Was there any means of exit from the rear of the dwelling?

Pollard did not know if there was or not, and he did not care to leave his post to investigate. He waited for a quarter of an hour, and he had moved to the edge of the pavement, and was looking up at the windows to see if there was a light at any of them, when he heard a shout from within the house, and immediately afterwards the report of a pistol.

There was another shout, and the sound of rapid footsteps. The door was thrown open, and a man appeared — an elderly man in pyjamas, with a pistol in his hand.

'Fetch a constable, young man!' he

cried, at sight of Pollard. 'Hurry!'

'What's wrong?' exclaimed Pollard.

'A burglar! I fired at him and missed!'

'What became of him?'

'He's gone! He escaped by the kitchen!'

'Is there a way out at the back?'

'Yes, a small yard. And beyond that an alley leading to Gosfield Street.'

It had been no burglar the man had fired at, Pollard was sure. He had promptly tumbled to the game, and as fast as he could he ran along Langham Street and round into Gosfield Street.

He had no more than turned the corner when he saw a man dart out from the mouth of the alley, twenty yards in front of him. The man was Edgar Creed, and he was carrying a kitbag.

He hastened to a taxi that was standing nearby and sprang into it. And the next instant the taxi was racing swiftly north.

There was not another one to be had. Pollard had been tricked and beaten, and as he retraced his steps he realised how the crook had prepared for flight.

'Confound the luck!' he said to himself. 'It was a clever dodge. I'll give Creed credit for that. When he went into the Tube station in Leicester Square he must have telephoned to somebody — probably to Marc Spartos — and asked him to send a taxi to the entrance to the alley in Gosfield Street, and tell the chauffeur to wait there.'

When the lad returned to Number 94 Langham Street, two constables had just come on the scene. They were standing in the open doorway, and the man in pyjamas was telling them, and several half-dressed lodgers who had hurried downstairs, what had happened.

'I am the landlord here,' he said. 'I sleep in a small room at the back of the house on the ground floor. I was roused by a noise, took my pistol from under my pillow, and got quietly out of bed. Then I slipped into the kitchen, and as soon as I switched on the light I saw a man with a bag in the act of opening the door. I fired at him, but the shot must have missed, for he ran into the yard and escaped. I suppose he has been stealing money and valuables from the rooms upstairs. I don't know yet if — '

'There has been no robbery,' Pollard interrupted. 'The man wasn't a burglar.'

'Of course he was,' declared the landlord. 'What do you know about it?'

'More than you think. You didn't see him clearly, I dare say.'

'No, I had only a glimpse of him.'

'You would have recognised him if you had seen his face. He was one of your lodgers.'

'One — one of my lodgers?'

'Yes, a fair man with a waxed moustache and a tuft of beard on his chin.'

'That is a description of Mr. Charles Mortimer, who has a front room on the second floor.'

'Well, I'll bet you he has disappeared.'

The landlord stared at the young man in bewilderment, and hastily ascended the stairs. He returned in a few moments.

'You are quite right!' he exclaimed. 'Mr. Mortimer is gone, and he has taken everything he had with him. I don't understand it. He paid me in advance for his room. There isn't anything owing!'

Pollard briefly explained.

'Mr. Mortimer is a crook, as it happens,' he said. 'I have been on his track tonight, and I shadowed him to Langham Street. He knew I was watching the house, and that is why he cleared out by the back.

'I am Lionel Crane's partner in disguise,' he added, turning to the two constables, 'and he gave me my instructions. I am not at liberty to say anything more.'

And with that, before the policemen could recover from their surprise, Pollard walked off. He picked up a taxi at Oxford Circus and drove home. Crane was not there, but he returned in the course of half an hour, and he was much disappointed when he heard Pollard's story.

'It is a great pity,' he said. 'You were not in the least to blame, though. You couldn't have been in two places at once.'

While speaking to Pollard on the telephone Crane had told him in a few words of the tragedy at the Hotel Dijon, and he now gave him a full account of the affair.

'We have got back to where we began,'

he continued, 'and we shall have to start afresh. George Harrap has the rubies, with the exception of the one he dropped in Burnley's bedroom. And Edgar Creed will certainly make every effort to find Harrap in spite of my warning. That is why I was so anxious to keep track of him.'

'We may learn something from the fingerprints,' said the young man, 'that will be helpful to us in searching for George Harrap.'

Crane nodded.

'It is possible,' he replied. 'They should have his record at Scotland Yard if he is a professional crook. And I haven't a doubt that he is.'

'Well, if Harrap hasn't any money, Li, he won't be able to get abroad unless he disposes of one of the rubies — or all of them.'

'He won't risk it. Not at present. And even if he had money he would be afraid to try to leave the country, knowing a strict watch will be set for him. He will hide in London.'

Though the case was at a standstill,

events were to move more quickly than Crane anticipated, and that owing to shrewd deductions on his part.

When he called at Scotland Yard the next day Inspector Pidgeon had enlightening news for him. The identities of George Harrap and John Burnley had been established. Duplicates of their fingerprints had readily been discovered in the records, showing that both men were professional criminals.

Harrap had been known in the past as Charles Grimper, and Burnley as Oscar Beckett. They had operated mostly in the big cities of the Midlands, committing burglaries on a large scale, and they had been twice sent to penal servitude.

A couple of years ago they had disappeared, and all trace of them had been lost. It was believed at the time, however, that they had gone to America, and with a considerable sum of money in their possession.

This information was useless to Crane. It could not be of any assistance to him in searching for a crook who had presumably not had any intimate friends in

London in the past, had been absent from England for a long period, and had only recently returned.

He was assured by Inspector Pidgeon that the police would be unremitting in their efforts to trace George Harrap, but he merely shrugged his shoulders in reply. He did not believe the police would succeed. He must rely on himself.

He was at a deadlock, however, and he went home chafing under a sense of impotency, yet doggedly determined that he would not be beaten.

What was he to do? Something must be done promptly, for the situation was as precarious as it was complicated. George Harrap had the rubies, and Edgar Creed knew it. He would search strenuously for the fugitive crook, and should he be the first to discover where he was — it was to be feared he would be — the rubies would be stolen again, and Harrap would probably be murdered. And Creed might then disappear with his plunder for good and all.

That was how matters stood, and Crane had reason to be apprehensive, as he told Pollard. One thing might be to his advantage, he pointed out. He had seen to it that there was no mention of the rubies, or of Harrap's name, in the newspaper account of the murder at the Hotel Dijon.

'It is a difficult proposition we have to deal with, Harry,' he continued. 'I am afraid that Edgar Creed, with his intimate knowledge of George Harrap, will be able to find him without much trouble. We must make every effort, therefore, to locate Creed, in the hope that by keeping him under surveillance we shall learn where Harrap is.'

'That's the idea,' said Pollard. 'What about the café in Bateman Street?'

'I have had that in mind,' Crane replied. 'I am pretty sure that Harrap won't visit the Café Spartos, disguised or otherwise. But in all probability Edgar Creed will do so, on the chance of finding Harrap there.'

'If he does he will be disguised, Li.'

'Yes, that goes without saying. He will be skilfully disguised, and he will be very much on his guard.'

Crane dropped the subject. He had been talking to the young man while they were at luncheon; and afterwards he settled down in his favourite chair by the fire, and sat there for a couple of hours, smoking numerous pipes of tobacco, not uttering a word.

He was absorbed in thought, trying to solve a difficult problem; and in the end he hit on a most ingenious scheme, which, he felt, would very likely be successful.

8

A Sensational Discovery

Between nine and ten o'clock that night a man of foreign appearance, with a swarthy complexion and a big, bushy moustache, strolled along Bateman Street, and slouched into the Café Spartos. His clothes were shabby, and he wore a black soft hat with a wide brim that drooped over his forehead.

He paused for a moment in the outer room, and, observing that there was no one in the one at the rear of the premises, he passed through to it, and seated himself at a small table.

He had been noticed by the proprietor, who followed him into the room, and regarded him suspiciously.

'You can't stay here,' he said gruffly. 'This place is for my regular customers only.'

'Well, I'm one of them,' the stranger quietly replied.

'Oh, no, you're not!' Marc Spartos declared. 'I've never laid eyes on you before! I dare say you're a police spy!'

'You are wrong, Spartos. I know I can trust you, else I wouldn't risk telling you who I am. The disguise is good, isn't it?'

'You are disguised — eh? I can't guess who — '

'I am George Harrap.'

'What — you're Harrap?'

'Yes, that's quite right.'

There was a moment of keen suspense for the shabby stranger, who was no other than Lionel Crane. It was possible, he had thought, that the real George Harrap might be in the café.

Clearly he was not, however. Otherwise Marc Spartos would have betrayed the fact by a quick change of countenance, whereas his expression showed merely a trace of uneasiness.

'I'll be with you in a minute,' he murmured.

He went to the bar, and when he returned with a bottle of wine and a couple of glasses, he sat down to the table, and poured out the wine.

'You're a fool, Harrap,' he said sharply. 'You shouldn't have come here. It's not safe for you, and it might get me into trouble. Though your name wasn't in the papers, there are plenty of people who know you did the murder at the Hotel Dijon in Long Acre.'

'Not a word of that,' bade George Harrap. 'I don't want to talk about it.'

'But I do,' Marc Spartos answered. 'Burnley was a friend of mine, and a decent sort. I've a good mind to detain you, and send for the police.'

'I'm not afraid of your doing that.'

'Why not?'

'Because I would split on you, for one thing. And what's more, I've come to discuss a matter of business that will be to your advantage.'

'To my advantage? What do you mean?'

'I will tell you presently,' said George Harrap. 'I want to know first if Edgar Creed has been here.'

For an instant Marc Spartos hesitated.

'No, I haven't seen anything of him for several days,' he replied.

'I don't believe it.'

'You can believe me or not. At all events, Creed isn't here now.'

'You know where he can be found, though.'

'Perhaps I do, and perhaps I don't. That is my business. What do you want with me, Harrap? Come to the point.'

George Harrap was silent for a few seconds. He lit a cigarette, and sipped his wine.

'I've got those rubies,' he said, at length, in a low tone.

'I know you have,' Marc Spartos whispered. 'What's that to me?'

'It depends,' said George Harrap. 'I am desperately anxious to get across to the Continent, and I need money. I am almost stony-broke. Will you buy one of the rubies? It is worth four thousand pounds, and you can have it for four hundred.'

Marc Spartos shook his head.

'I should be afraid to touch it,' he replied. 'The stones are too widely known.'

'You could keep it until it was safe to dispose of it. Why not? Suppose I knock a hundred off the price? I'll let it go for three hundred.'

'I might be willing to pay that for it, though I'm short of ready money myself. Have you got the ruby with you, Harrap?'

'No, it is hidden at my place with the rest of them.'

'What is the address? Where are you living?'

'I wouldn't tell you or anybody that. Not likely. But it's no great distance from here. I can fetch the ruby if you'll buy it.'

'I will think it over,' said Marc Spartos. 'Don't go yet. I will be back shortly. I must finish the work I was doing when you came in.'

He rose and returned to his desk at one end of the bar. That he had been deceived was obvious. But would Crane accomplish his object? He was strongly inclined to think he would. It depended on whether or not the Greek was in touch with Edgar Creed.

If so, and Creed was in the café tonight, Spartos would almost certainly let him know that Harrap was here. And, should Creed not be here, Spartos would promptly get word to him.

'I believe it will be all right,' Crane reflected. 'I shall land my fish. The Greek knows it will be more to his advantage to stand in with Edgar Creed than with George Harrap.'

Marc Spartos was writing at the desk. Presently he beckoned to Alphonse, the French waiter, and spoke a few words to him; then added loudly enough for Crane to hear:

'It is on one of the shelves in my bedroom. You can't mistake it. An account-book bound in red.'

The waiter came to the inner room, and disappeared through a door that gave access to the staircase. At the foot of the stairs, as Crane knew, was a door which led to a side street; and, listening with strained ears, he heard that door softly opened and closed. It was as he had expected. There could be no doubt that Alphonse had been sent to give a message to Edgar Creed.

In the course of twenty minutes, Alphonse returned. He went to the bar, and told the Greek, in an audible voice, that he had not been able to find the book.

Marc Spartos swore at him, and called him a stupid fool; and a few moments later he came back to the inner room, and sat down to the table.

'I've decided to take your offer, Harrap,' he said. 'I will give you three hundred pounds for the ruby. Not tonight, though. I haven't got the money.'

'You will have it tomorrow?' George Harrap asked.

'Yes, I will draw it from the bank.'

'Very well. I will be here at eleven o'clock with the stone. And now I'll be off. This isn't a healthy place for me.'

Both men rose, and Crane left the café with an easy mind, satisfied that Edgar Creed had received a description of him from Alphonse, and was waiting somewhere outside.

He was careful not to glance about him. He bore to the right along Bateman Street, and just before he turned into Dean Street he passed a shabby youth who was lighting a cigarette.

The youth was Pollard, and he had lit

the cigarette to indicate to Crane that somebody was following him.

The game was on. At a leisurely pace Crane struck down to Piccadilly Circus, and then by the Haymarket and Whitehall to Westminster Bridge. He had not once looked behind him, nor did he do so as he crossed the bridge, and walked along the Westminster Bridge Road.

He turned into King Edward Street, and a little farther on he turned again into a narrow thoroughfare that was dark and deserted.

A taxi was waiting here, close beyond the corner, and the door was open. Crane whipped quickly inside, and the cab started off before he had shut the door.

And now, as he glanced back, he had a glimpse of a tall man with a bushy beard that was split in the middle.

He had arranged beforehand for this means of getting rid of his pursuer. It was by his instructions the taxi had been waiting here. He had done his part, and it remained for Pollard to do the rest.

Oddly enough, the man with the beard was apparently not much disappointed.

He shrugged his shoulders, and gazed after the receding cab for a moment; and as he retraced his steps to the Westminster Bridge Road he was shadowed by Pollard, who had dogged him from Soho.

The man was not on his guard. He had no reason to suspect that a trap had been set for him. He got into a bus near the bridge, and Pollard climbed to the top of it.

Both descended at Piccadilly Circus, and, still followed by the young man, the man walked leisurely along Shaftesbury Avenue, and up Dean Street.

And now, certain that he knew where his quarry was going, Pollard did a clever thing. By way of Old Compton Street and Frith Street he hastened to the east end of Bateman Street, turned the corner, and slouched into the Café Spartos.

There were only four or five customers here at this hour, and they were close to the door. The young man chose a table that was at one side of the outer room and opposite to the bar; and when Alphonse had brought him a glass of wine he leaned back against the wall in an attitude that suggested that he was the worse for drink, and half-closed his eyes.

He had not made a mistake. Very soon the door was opened, and the man with the split beard entered the café. He seated himself at a table that was within four yards of Pollard, and almost at once Marc Spartos came over to him, and sat down by his side. And then the young man, listening intently, heard the first words that were uttered.

'You've been a long while,' said the Greek, in a low tone. 'What luck?'

'I lost the fellow, confound him!' the other answered. 'He gave me the slip. It doesn't matter, though. I learned enough to be sure that he was playing a cunning game.'

'Where did you lose him, Harrap?'

'He jumped into a taxi near the Westminster Bridge Road.'

Harrap! Pollard barely stifled an exclamation that rose to his lips. So both he and Crane had been deceived! The man with the split beard, whom he had shadowed in the belief that he was Edgar Creed disguised, was no other than

George Harrap! The murderer of John Burnley! The man who had the rubies in his possession!

It was a thrilling discovery, and it would have important results should the young man succeed in finding out where the crook lived.

'My word, it will be good news for Li!' he reflected.

For a few moments he was unable to hear what the men were talking about, and then his keen ears caught more of the conversation, though it was carried on almost in whispers.

'There can't be any doubt, I suppose,' said George Harrap, 'that the fellow who impersonated me was Edgar Creed?'

'He couldn't have been anybody else,' Marc Spartos replied.

'It was a daring game — eh?'

'Yes, he ran a big risk. He took the chance of you being in the café. I dare say he suspected you had been here since the murder, and he thought I might know your address. Or perhaps it was in his mind, before he pitched me the yarn, that you would be here in disguise, and he

121

could spot you. He wants the rubies badly, and he would murder you to get them.'

George Harrap nodded. 'I don't understand it,' he declared. 'What you have just told me doesn't account for Creed playing such a trick. What had he to gain by it?'

'To get on your track, of course,' the Greek answered.

'I'm not so sure. There is something queer about it all.'

'Something queer? What do you mean?'

'I've been thinking that the man may have been Lionel Crane. It would be like him.'

'Nonsense! Put that idea out of your head. Lionel Crane wouldn't have come to the café unless he had thought you might be here, and if he had thought that he would not have impersonated you. That stands to reason, doesn't it?'

'Yes, it does,' George Harrap assented. 'You are right. The man must have been Creed. I wish I knew where he was living. I want to find him.'

'I would like to know myself,' the

Greek replied, with an odd glance at his companion.

'What for?'

'He owes me some money, Harrap. What do you want with him?'

'I would do him in, curse him! He served Burnley and me dirty.'

The conversation was continued in such low tones that Pollard could not hear any of it. He strained his ears, and at length George Harrap raised his voice, and said audibly:

'It is a sure thing for tomorrow night, then? Twelve o'clock?'

'Twelve o'clock sharp,' Marc Spartos answered.

'You will have the money ready?'

'You can depend on that. But you must bring all of the rubies with you. I want to choose from them.'

'Right you are, Spartos.'

Pollard now concluded that it was time for him to leave. He could not expect to get any more information. He sat up, and stretched his arms and yawned, as if he had been asleep; and then, having emptied his wine glass, he rose from the table, threw a drowsy glance around him; and lurched unsteadily out to the street.

He crossed to the other side and slipped into a dark doorway, and as he stood there he saw a man with a heavy moustache go into the Café Spartos. And that man, as it happened, was Edgar Creed.

He had hardly more than entered when George Harrap appeared, and, turning towards Dean Street, he walked down that thoroughfare, warily shadowed by the young man.

The chase led to Piccadilly Circus, and there it abruptly terminated. The crook went across to Swan & Edgar's Corner, and, quickening his steps, he got on to a 'bus that was just moving off. The 'bus was full up A couple of men ran after it, and stopped as the conductor shook his head at them.

It was the hour when people were flocking from the theatres, and there was not a taxi to be had. Nor was there another 'bus approaching.

Pollard had lost his quarry. It was not much of a disappointment to him, however. No great harm had been done, he felt, as he recalled the final part of the conversation he had heard at the Café Spartos.

'It is all right,' he said to himself. 'We shall land George Harrap tomorrow night, and the rubies as well.'

He stood on the corner for a few moments, and then, unable to get either a 'bus or a cab he walked up Regent Street. At Oxford Circus he got a taxi, and drove home.

Crane had been there for some little time and he listened in amazement to the long story the young man told him — listened with increasing interest that culminated in a dramatic surprise.

'George Harrap!' he exclaimed. 'The very man we are after! The man with the rubies! It was he who shadowed me in the belief that I was Edgar Creed, and I was under the impression that he was Creed! How cunningly that scoundrel Spartos played his part! Not by the faintest sign did he betray the fact that he knew me to be an impostor! So George Harrap has fallen into the net! Nothing could be more fortunate than the way things have turned out! We have been saved a lot of trouble! Our task is nearly finished, Harry, thanks to those keen ears of yours!'

Continuing, Crane related his experience at the Café Spartos, and briefly repeated his conversation with the Greek.

'My stratagem has been a complete success, better than I anticipated,' he went on. 'I did not think that Harrap was in touch with Spartos. He is going to make a deal in rubies with him, is he? He wants to raise money so he can escape to the Continent, of course. Well and good. He will have a startling surprise tomorrow night. It is of no importance to us where he is living, since we know of his appointment.'

'You will have him arrested when he arrives at the café, I suppose?' said Pollard.

Crane shook his head.

'Most certainly not,' he declared. 'Where are your wits? Wool-gathering?'

'What do you mean, Li? Why not arrest George Harrap before he goes in? He will have all of the rubies with him. He told the Greek so.'

'I am sure he won't. Quite sure. He is anything but a fool. He won't run the risk of being robbed of all his spoils. He will bring one of the stones with him, or perhaps two. We will wait until he leaves, and follow him to his lodgings, have him arrested there, and recover the rubies. That is what we will do.'

'We will have to be careful that he doesn't give us the slip, as he did me tonight.'

'We will guard against that, Harry.'

Crane paused for a moment.

'We may be able to kill two birds with one stone, so to speak,' he added. 'I would like to get Marc Spartos into the clutches of the law, and put an end to his career of villainy. He has had a long stretch of it.'

9

The Death of Marc Spartos

Lionel Crane and Pollard were lurking in the vicinity, on the alert, when, at twelve o'clock on the following night, George Harrap came along a narrow passage that ran north from Bateman Street.

He rapped softly on the side door of the Café Spartos, and it was opened almost immediately by the Greek, who had been waiting in the dark hall.

He shut and locked the door, and with a hand on Harrap's arm, to guide his steps in the pitch darkness, he led him to the top of the stairs, and from the landing into a room that was on the first floor and at the rear of the premises.

It was a cosily furnished room, and in the middle of it was a large table on which were bottles and glasses, and a box of cigars. A pair of heavy draperies were drawn across the one window.

The men sat down to the table. Marc Spartos pushed the cigar-box over to his companion, and filled two small glasses with brandy.

'It is good stuff,' he said. 'It will cheer you up.'

'I need some cheering,' George Harrap moodily replied. 'It's been nothing but worry and trouble since I got back from Burma, what with Edgar Creed playing his dirty game, and Lionel Crane trying to get on my track. I'll not feel safe until I am on the other side of the Channel. By the way, have you seen anything of Creed since last night?'

'No, he's not been to the café. He is afraid to come. He must know I tumbled to his trick. But let us get to business. I have the money. Where are the rubies? You have brought them with you?'

'I have brought one of them.'

'Only — only one, Harrap?'

'Yes, the best of the lot.'

The Greek stared in dismay.

'You were to have brought all of them!' he snapped. 'You told me you would.'

'I didn't promise!' George Harrap answered.

'Well, you can go to your lodgings and fetch the rest. I want to make my own choice.'

'No, Spartos, I won't. I'm not a fool.'

'You think you can't trust me, eh?'

'I'm not sure. At all events, I'm not giving you a chance to rob me of a fortune. Show me the money, and I'll show you the ruby I brought. It is yours for three hundred pounds.'

'I've half a mind to call the deal off Harrap.'

'You won't do that. I am offering you the biggest kind of a bargain.'

Marc Spartos hesitated, scowling at the crook. He placed a sheaf of banknotes on the table, and George Harrap produced the glittering stone. The Greek took if from him, held it to the light, and slipped it into his pocket.

'The money is yours!' he said. 'And now have another drink.'

The last words were meant for a signal, and at once a door opposite to the crook was quietly opened and a man stepped out from an adjoining room — a tall man, with a pointed beard.

Seating himself at the table, he whisked off his false beard, drew a pistol, and pointed it at George Harrap, who was speechless with consternation for a moment.

'Creed!' he gasped. 'You — you here!'

Edgar Creed smiled grimly.

'Don't stir!' he bade. 'Put your hands in front of you, and sit still!'

The crook, who had meanwhile thrust the banknotes into his pocket, obeyed the command. He glared at Edgar Creed, and looked from him to the Greek, trembling with rage.

'You dirty traitor!' he snarled. 'You've double-crossed me!'

Marc Spartos laughed.

'That's right!' he assented. 'It was to my advantage. Creed happened to drop in last night just as you were leaving, and we fixed things between us. Instead of getting one of the rubies, I am going to have a share of them.'

'Are you, though? I can't see you doing it, Spartos!'

'I can. You are in the tightest kind of a trap, and we mean to put the screws on you.'

Edgar Creed's automatic was still pointed at the crook.

'Yes, we've got you in a tight place, Harrap,' he said. 'You can't grumble. It is no more than you deserve. You tried to kill me, and you murdered John Burnley. And you are going to pay for it by losing every damned ruby. I know where you are living. Spartos has given me the address. But no doubt you have very skilfully hidden the stones at your lodgings. I might not be able to find them, so you must tell me exactly where they are.'

'I'll never tell you!' George Harrap declared. 'Hanged if I will!'

'You will, and without delay. You'll have only one chance. We won't waste time in arguing. If you refuse, we will fetch the police here, and charge you with the murder.'

'There — there isn't any evidence against me!'

'There is plenty of evidence. You will be hanged, and Spartos and I will get the reward that has been offered for the recovery of the rubies.'

'Can I have half of them if I tell you where they are?'

'No, not one of them. And you are not going to keep the money Spartos gave you, either. Out with it.'

The crook was silent, breathing hard, his fists clenched convulsively. He was in a white fury. There was a devilish glitter in his eyes.

Edgar Creed was watching him like a hawk.

'The money!' he said. 'Give it to Spartos!'

'He don't get it,' George Harrap replied. 'He has one of the rubies.'

'Yes, and we mean to have the rest of them. Tell us where they are hidden. Or would you rather be arrested?'

'I'll — I'll tell you, curse you! There is nothing else for it!'

'Ah, that's sensible of you! Where are the stones?'

'They are at my lodgings, concealed in the bed. If you rip open the lower end of the mattress — '

As George Harrap spoke he suddenly jumped up, and, at the same time, he bore his weight so heavily against the table that it was overturned with a crash, hurling both Edgar Creed and the Greek to the floor.

They lay sprawling amongst broken glasses and bottles, struggling to rise; and as they scrambled to their feet, cursing with rage, the frenzied crook jerked a pistol from his pocket.

There was a sharp report, a jet of flame. Marc Spartos screamed horribly, and clutched at his chest, staggered, and pitched to the floor again.

Edgar Creed fired his automatic at Harrap, and, missing him in his haste, he fired a second shot. The bullet struck Harrap's pistol, knocking it from his grasp as he was about to discharge it; and the next instant, as a third shot grazed his shoulder, he leapt at Creed and dealt him a smashing blow that sent him reeling to the wall, where he stumbled over a chair and fell.

He was out of action for the moment, and the Greek was lying motionless by the table.

It had all occurred in the space of a few seconds, and now, bent on escape, George Harrap picked up his automatic, and made a dash for the door that led to the staircase.

He tore it open, turned round and fired two shots at Edgar Creed. And, without waiting to see if he had hit him or not, he took to flight.

★   ★   ★

Lionel Crane and Pollard were standing in a dark doorway opposite to the main entrance to the Café Spartos when they faintly heard the crash of the falling table, and then the rapid fusillade of pistol-shots.

They raced over to the café, and were at once joined by two constables who had been nearby, and had also heard the firing.

It had ceased now. At a word from Crane the young man hastened round into the narrow passage that skirted the building, and he had no more than reached the side door when it was thrown open, and George Harrap darted out. He sprang at Pollard and knocked him down with one blow, then took to his heels, running towards Oxford Street.

The young man was not much hurt. He got to his feet as quickly as he could, and at the same moment Edgar Creed rushed out of the house. He had not replaced his false beard, and, recognising him at sight, Pollard pluckily grappled with him.

There was a brief struggle, and it ended disastrously for Pollard who was a trifle dazed by the blow he had received from Harrap, and was no match for the second crook.

His grip was easily broken. Once more he was knocked down, and when he scrambled to his feet again, feeling very groggy, he saw that George Harrap had disappeared and had a glimpse of Creed fading into the darkness in the same direction in which Harrap had gone.

Meanwhile, there had been sounds of pounding and hammering in Bateman Street, and now Crane came on the scene hurrying along the passage with a pistol in his hand.

'Ah here you are!' he said breathlessly. 'The police have forced open the front door of the café! They are going through

136

the bar! We will enter by the — ' He paused abruptly. 'You have been fighting!' he exclaimed. 'Who with?'

'With George Harrap!' Pollard replied. 'He got away from me! And afterwards I had a fight with Edgar Creed!'

'With Edgar Creed? He has been in the building, too, Harry?'

'That's right, Li!' They are both gone, in the direction of Oxford Street! I couldn't help it!'

'So Creed and Harrap have slipped through our fingers! It is most unfortunate!'

'It wouldn't be any use to search for them,' said Pollard. 'They have a good start. We had better see what has happened inside. Somebody may have been shot.'

'The Greek, I am afraid,' Crane answered. 'Nothing has been seen of him, and all is quiet.'

The alarm had spread throughout the neighbourhood, and Bateman Street was ringing with the excited voices of many people. As Crane and the young man went into the house by the side door one of the constables appeared from the bar — the other was guarding the front entrance — and, hearing no sound above them, the three ascended the stairs, and entered the lighted room off the landing.

It was a startling sight that met their eyes.

Crane's gaze swept the disordered room observing the bullet-holes in the walls — the overturned table — the litter of broken glasses drenched with spilt wine and brandy — and the huddled form of Marc Spartos lying amongst the debris.

'He is dead!' cried Pollard. 'Another murder, Li!'

But the Greek was not dead. There was life in his unconscious body, though he had been shot in the chest. He was lifted on to a couch, and Crane bared his breast, and looked at the wound.

'It will prove fatal,' he declared. 'There isn't any hope. The man can't live very long, I am sure. I hope we will be able to pull him round. It is important that he should be questioned.'

He told Pollard to fetch a doctor who

lived in the vicinity. The young man hurried off on his errand, and the constable went down to the bar, and returned with a bottle of brandy and a glass. When a quantity of the strong spirit had been poured between the Greek's lips he moaned and stirred, and a tinge of colour crept into his pallid cheeks.

It was not until the doctor had arrived however, that he was brought back to consciousness. Crane had meanwhile searched his pockets, and had discovered the ruby, which indicated that his deductions had been correct.

The doctor placed on a chair a black bag he had brought with him, and sitting down by the side of the Greek, he made a thorough examination of the wound, and shook his head.

'I can't do anything for him,' he declared, 'and it would not be worth while to remove him to a hospital, for he can't live more than half an hour at the most.'

Marc Spartos had relapsed into a state of coma. Already there was an ominous rattling in his throat. He was lifted up, with his back against the end of the couch and another drink of brandy revived him. He opened his eyes, and gazed about the room.

'Am — am I dying?' he muttered, in a husky whisper.

'Yes, you will die very soon,' Crane replied. 'Nothing can be done for you. Tell us while you can what happened here tonight. There were two men with you, George Harrap and Edgar Creed. And Harrap came to sell you one of the rubies that he and John Burnley stole in Burma.'

The Greek nodded.

'I'll tell the whole truth,' he said, in a weak voice. 'There was a quarrel. Creed and I meant to rob Harrap. We thought he would have all the rubies with him, but he had only one. We tried to make him tell us where he had hidden the rest, and he refused. He suddenly threw the table over, hurling us to the floor. Then he drew a pistol, and fired at me — and that's all I remember.'

'You paid Harrap for the ruby you got from him?'

'Yes, three hundred pounds in bank-notes.'

'Do you know where both men have been living, Spartos?'

'Not Creed. He never told me.'

'And Harrap?' asked Crane. 'Where are his lodgings?'

'They are in Pollen Street, Hanover Square,' Marc Spartos answered.

'What number? Tell me!'

'I — I think it is — '

'The number? Be quick!'

'I am trying to — remember — but — but — '

The Greek's voice was choked by a flow of blood to his mouth. He lifted himself, struggling for breath; dropped back, and lay quite still. He was dead. The fatal rubies had cost another life. And Marc Spartos had died before he could tell what he knew, before he could recall the number on which so much depended.

Crane turned to Pollard.

'How far was Creed behind Harrap when they took to flight?' he inquired.

'I haven't any clear idea,' the young man replied. 'I had a dim glimpse of

Creed running when I got up after he had knocked me down.'

'You think he may have been able to keep Harrap in sight?'

'Very likely, Li. Both ran in the same direction, and Harrap hadn't much of a start on Creed.'

Another failure! Fresh complications! Crane's disappointment was keen. He had been baffled again. Again the triumph he had anticipated had been snatched from his grasp.

His mind worked swiftly. Since the Greek knew where George Harrap lived, it was to be presumed that he had told Edgar Creed.

It could scarcely be doubted that he had. On the other hand, had Creed not known the address, he had in all probability kept track of Harrap; caught sight of him, and shadowed him.

It had been Harrap's intention, of course, to hurry to his lodgings, get the rubies, and find another lodging. Had he succeeded in getting away with his plunder? If so, had Creed followed him from Pollen Street? Or had he by now

142

murdered Harrap, and stolen the rubies? Be which it may, it was to be feared that the rubies might never be recovered.

And there was another thing to be taken into consideration. Harrap had three hundred pounds in his possession, and, in the event of his eluding Creed, he would make every effort to escape to the Continent.

'Be off at once,' Crane said to Pollard, after brief reflection. 'Pollen Street is a very short thoroughfare. There are not many houses. You may be able to learn by inquiries where Harrap has been lodging. Possibly he is still there, and Creed is watching the place. Do your best. If you should see anything of Harrap shadow him, and have him arrested at the first opportunity, for he will have the rubies with him. I will come on later, Harry. I shan't be very long.'

Pollard hastily departed, and soon afterwards, as Crane was about to leave, a Bow Street inspector who had heard of the murder entered the room.

This delayed Crane. He had to give the inspector a full account of the crime, making everything clear to him; and thus it happened that a considerable time had elapsed when at last he left the Café Spartos, pushed through the crowd that was gathered in Bateman Street, and sought for a taxi.

10

The Man in the Dark

It would have been taken for granted, by persons unfamiliar with the byways of the West End of London, that a man who lived in the near vicinity of Hanover Square must have some means.

That was not the case with Pollen Street, however. One could live very cheaply in this short, very narrow, and choked thoroughfare, which was parallel with Regent Street, and ran from fashionable Hanover Street to fashionable Maddox Street.

The dwellings were tall and dingy, and in need of paint. There were a number of inexpensive little shops occupied by petty tradesmen — a greengrocer, a dairyman, a cobbler, an oil and colour merchant, a draper and a pastry cook. And there was also a tiny beerhouse kept by a retired constable of the name of Jim Yardley, who had formerly been attached to the Marylebone Division, and was acquainted with Lionel Crane and his young partner.

The place was closed for the night, but Jim Yardley was smoking a pipe in a doorway next to the bar — a door that led to his living room above — when Pollard strolled down Pollen Street from the direction of Hanover Street.

'Hello, young man!' Yardley said. 'What are you doing in this quarter at such an hour? Detective work — eh?'

'That's right,' Pollard replied. 'A little matter of business for Crane. I'm on a hot scent.'

'A hot scent in Pollen Street? You won't find a crook from one end of it to the other.'

'Don't you believe it! I'm on the track of one of the biggest scoundrels in London. A thief and a murderer. Perhaps you can help me. How, long have you been standing here?'

'For something like twenty minutes.'

'And nothing exciting has happened, Jim?'

'Nothing more exciting than a dog fight.'

'Well, it's like this,' Pollard continued. 'The man I want has been living in Pollen Street. I know that for a certainty, but I don't know the number. Can you tell me if any new lodger has taken a room in the street recently?'

Jim Yardley stroked his chin.

'I know everybody,' he answered, 'and there has been only one strange face. I first noticed the man about a week ago, when he dropped into my bar for a drink. I got into conversation with him, and he told me his name was Watson, and he was a printer out of a job. He has been in several times since. I don't like his looks. He has eyes like a fish, sort of cold and sinister.'

'You know what house he lodges in?'

'Yes, nearly opposite, at No. 12. I've seen him go in and come out, and once I saw him at one of the windows of the front room on the third floor.'

'Have you seen him tonight?' asked the young man.

'No, I haven't laid eyes on him,' Jim Yardley replied.

'Have you seen any person lurking about, watching that house?'

'No one, young man. As for the party I've been speaking of, I dare say he is in bed. There isn't a light in his room.'

Jim Yardley's statements pointed to a definite conclusion. If the man lodging at No. 12 was the only stranger who had recently come to live in Pollen Street, that man must be George Harrap.

Had he been afraid to return to his lodgings tonight, and gone somewhere else? On the other hand, had he come back to get the rubies, and taken flight with them? And, in that event, had he been followed here by Edgar Creed, or had he thrown him off his track?

Or was Harrap over there now, fearing to venture out? If so, where was Creed? Was he too, in the house, waiting and watching as a savage tiger waits for its prey? There was no sign of him in Pollen Street. Possibly he had murdered Harrap in his room, stolen the rubies, and made his escape.

As Harrap had a large amount of money, and would lose no time in trying to get abroad, it was of vital importance that Pollard should promptly ascertain just how matters stood.

'I'm going into that house if I can,' he said. 'I've got to find out if my man is there or not. I wonder if the door is locked?'

'It is never locked,' Jim Yardley answered. 'The lodgers aren't afraid of burglars, as they have nothing worth stealing. But perhaps the man Watson isn't the one you are after.'

'He is. I am sure of it,' declared Pollard.

'You will be running a risk, then. Hadn't I better go with you?'

'No, I had rather go alone. I'll be careful.'

'And if you should get into trouble?'

'I'll shout for help, Jim. You stay where you are for awhile.'

'Very well. I'll wait here until you come out. You can count on me should you need assistance.'

There was no light at any of the front windows of No. 12. Pollard glided across, and, finding the door ajar, he pushed it open, and slipped into the hall.

He was in pitch darkness. Not the faintest sound came to his ears. Yet the very silence was ominous, he felt. Something seemed to tell him that deadly peril lurked above.

But he did not hesitate. His courage did not falter. He groped to the staircase, and with stealthy tread, grasping the banister, he slowly mounted to the first floor, found the second flight of stairs, and as warily ascended to the second floor, where he paused.

Still there was no sound. His apprehensions were somewhat lulled. He would venture higher. He must. Above him was the third and top floor, and it was there, he knew, that George Harrap had been lodging.

He crept to the staircase, and when he had put his foot on it he stopped abruptly, giving a quick start. What was that? His ears had just caught a rustling noise, and it had not come from in front of him.

He turned round, and as he listened, with his heart pounding against his ribs, he heard heavy breathing. He was frightened now. His escape was cut off. Somebody was standing close behind him, invisible in the dark.

Was it Harrap, or was it Creed? Doubtless it was one or the other. The crisis called for swift action.

Pollard did not wait to be attacked, did not wait to draw his pistol. Clenching his fist, he drove it into the gloom with all his strength, and struck solid flesh and bone. As he whipped back, prepared to deal another blow, there was a gasping cry, followed by a clattering crash. A moan, and hushed silence again. Not a sound.

The young man pulled an electric torch from his pocket, and flashed it beneath him. The silvery beam shone full on the face of Edgar Creed. He was lying a little way down the stairs in a huddled heap, stunned or dead, perhaps with a broken neck.

Had he been above? Had murder been done? No, from the position Creed had been in when he was struck he must have been ascending from below. He must have shadowed George Harrap from Soho to Pollen Street, and it was certain, therefore, that Harrap was in his room, and that he had not been robbed of the rubies.

This logical view had no more than occurred to Pollard, greatly to his relief, when he was startled by a noise somewhere overhead. He switched off the torch, and looked up.

He heard somebody moving; heard creaking, crackling sounds, and another sound that was like the harsh rasping of a bolt thrust from its socket. He saw a trapdoor in the roof lifted, and by a dim patch of light saw the black figure of a man squeeze through it.

The trap fell with a dull thud, and again all was darkness. The man was George Harrap of course. He had hurried from his room as soon as he heard the crash, and, fearing that Edgar Creed was down there, and had stumbled on the staircase, he had taken to flight from above. He was gone, and it could not be doubted that he had the rubies with him.

Swiftly this flashed to Pollard's mind, and with not an instant's delay he rapidly ascended the stairs to the top floor, his torch in his hand. He played the light in front of him, and it showed him a perpendicular ladder against the wall at the rear of the landing.

Up he went, as fast as he could climb; and when he had raised the trapdoor, and scrambled through it on to the flat roof of the dwelling, he saw George Harrap running a short distance beyond him.

'Ah, there you go!' he cried. 'You're for it now, you blighter! You're as good as caught!'

He had better have held his tongue. The man looked back, and ran the faster, with Pollard in hot pursuit. The two raced over the roof, leapt a few feet onto a lower roof, and sped across that; while the young man, who was gaining, shouted loudly at intervals.

At length Harrap stopped and whipped round, and levelled a pistol. There was a jet of flame, and a bullet hummed by Pollard's ear. The crook pulled the trigger again, and there was no report. His weapon was empty, and with an oath he continued his flight.

'I'll try to cripple him,' Pollard

reflected. 'He may get away if I don't.'

He raised his automatic, and fired twice, aiming low. Both shots missed. He fired a third shot, and missed again. Harrap ran on, and a couple of strides brought him to the edge of the roof, where he suddenly vanished, apparently jumping into space.

He had not done so, however. Pollard hastened to the spot, gazed beneath him, and saw the crook descending by a fire-escape, still in plain view.

The young man immediately followed, reckless of what danger might await him in that dizzy, yawning gulf that was shrouded in darkness. Where the fire escape led to he did not know.

He took it rapidly, climbing down at such a speed that he was in imminent peril of his life; swaying over the handrails, whirling sharply around corners, and swinging precariously from stairway to stairway, from platform to platform.

And at length, when he was nearly at the bottom, he saw below him a paved yard enclosed by three blank walls, and a fourth wall with windows and a door.

And he also saw George Harrap at a window next to the door — saw him smash it to fragments with the butt-end of his pistol — and saw him disappear through it.

A moment later Pollard leapt from the last platform to the yard, and dashing to the shattered window, he clutched the sill, swung himself over, and dropped into a big shop where a feeble jet of gas was burning.

The dim, speeding figure of the crook was visible beyond him. He fired his automatic twice, aiming hurriedly, and fired again. It was his last cartridge, and he had not hit Harrap, who had now reached the front door, and was fumbling at it. In a trice he had it open, and was gone.

After him went Pollard, and as he rushed out of the shop, to see at a glance that he was in Maddox Street, he had a glimpse of the crook running round the corner of Mill Street with somebody in chase of him.

He joined in the pursuit, but had not

taken three strides when a constable sprang at him from one side, and seized him by the collar.

'Got you, my fine fellow!' he exclaimed.

Pollard knew the man.

'It's all right, Martin!' he cried. 'Let me go! I'm after a crook! A thief and a murderer!'

'Of course you are!' jeered the constable, as he snatched the young man's pistol from him. 'Tell that tale to the marines! You've been doing a burglary — you and your accomplice!'

'But I've told you the truth! Let me go! I'm Lionel Crane's partner.'

'Lionel Crane's what? That's a good one that is!'

'I am! I swear I am, Martin! I'm Pollard in disguise! I've got a lot of greasepaint on!'

'You've got a lot of nerve to pitch me such a yarn! Keep quiet, or I'll hit you with my truncheon!'

The constable was not to be convinced. He kept a tight grip of the young man, who soon quieted down, realising that he would have to make the best of it.

Meanwhile, the alarm had spread through the neighbourhood. An excited crowd had gathered. People were running from all directions, and others were gazing from windows on both sides of the street. More constables came on the scene, and they were talking to Pollard's captor when the report of a pistol was faintly heard above the clamour.

'Ah, that was a shot!' declared Constable Martin. 'It must have been either Drewitt or the crook who fired.'

'It wasn't the crook,' said Pollard. 'His pistol was empty.'

'Who's Drewitt, Martin?' one of the other constables inquired. 'You mean the C.I.D. man?'

'Yes, he's been with me in plain clothes tonight,' was the reply.

Pollard was elated. He had little or no doubt that George Harrap had been caught, dead or alive, and if so the rubies would be recovered. He made another effort to convince the constable who had arrested him of his identity.

'I am only thinly disguised, Martin.' he said. 'Jim Yardley, who has the little bar in

Pollen Street, recognised me at once, and I wonder you didn't. Yardley has seen a lot more of me than you have, though.'

While he was speaking the crowd had started to make way for a taxi that was approaching from the direction of Regent Street. It stopped now, in front of the haberdashery shop through which the crook had escaped, and Lionel Crane stepped out of it.

'Ah, here you are, Harry!' he exclaimed. 'What's the trouble?'

Constable Martin stared at him in bewilderment. 'Is — is this really — Pollard, sir?' he asked.

'Certainly, Martin.'

'Well I'm blowed! I'm very sorry, Mr. Crane. I've had him in custody. I thought he was a crook.'

Crane was not in a mood to laugh at the mistake. It was obvious to him that things had gone wrong. He questioned Pollard, who briefly related all that had happened, stating also that it was a C.I.D. man who had given chase to George Harrap, and that he had fired at him a little while ago.

'We had better look for Drewitt, Li,' he continued. 'He hasn't returned yet. And then we must see what has become of Edgar Creed. I hope he is still lying unconscious on the staircase.'

Jim Yardley now put in an appearance, and before he could utter a word a fresh clamour was heard at no great distance. It swelled louder, coming from somewhere to the south of Maddox Street.

Crane and the young man glanced at each other uneasily, and set off at once, accompanied by Yardley and the constables.

Guided by shouts, and by the repeated shrilling of a police-whistle, they hastened round to Mill Street and down that narrow thoroughfare, across Conduit Street, and through the short passage that led to Savile Row, where they pushed into a noisy crowd that had assembled.

Stretched on the pavement, just outside the entrance to the passage, was the body of a man, and Crane saw at first sight that it was not George Harrap.

'Good heavens, it's Drewitt!' Constable Martin cried in horror. 'The poor fellow has been murdered!'

He was right. Leonard Drewitt, one of the best men attached to the Criminal Investigation Department, was dead. He had been shot through the heart, and at such close range that his coat was scorched where the bullet had penetrated it.

Constable Martin turned to Pollard. 'You told me the crook's pistol was empty,' he said.

'So it was,' the young man replied. 'He fired half a dozen shots while I was chasing him. He didn't reload afterwards, so he couldn't have had any more cartridges.'

'Drewitt must have been shot with his own pistol,' said Crane, 'and Harrap carried it off. It isn't here.'

There had been no witnesses of the tragedy, it appeared. No one had seen and pursued the murderer. But it was an easy matter to reconstruct what had occurred.

Leonard Drewitt had been in hot chase of the crook, his automatic in his hand; and Harrap, finding that his pursuer was gaining on him, had whipped round the corner as soon as he emerged from the passage into Savile Row, waited, and flung himself upon the C.I.D. man.

The two had struggled, and either Drewitt's weapon had been accidentally discharged, or the crook had wrenched it from his grasp and shot him.

The latter theory was probably correct. Be that as it may, yet another life had paid toll to the curse of the fatal rubies. Crimson jewels that left a crimson wake of blood! Did the spirit of some malevolent demon lurk in their glittering depths?

Crane's disappointment was too bitter for words. Once more he had been cheated of success, and he would have to begin all over again. He had lost George Harrap, and Harrap, escaped into the vast maze of London, had the rubies with him. Would they ever be recovered?

'We'll get Creed, perhaps,' said Pollard. 'I suppose you want him, Li?'

'I want him badly,' Crane answered. 'If he should be arrested on a charge of being concerned in the affair at the Café

Spartos he won't have a chance to search for Harrap.'

Leaving the police at the scene of the tragedy, they slipped away unobserved, and Jim Yardley went with them.

'No, I didn't see anybody come out of the house while I was waiting for Pollard,' he said in reply to a question from Crane, as they were hurrying round to Pollen Street. 'Your man may be still there.'

The secluded little thoroughfare was quiet and deserted. The dwellings could not have been roused by the firing on the roofs. With a pistol in one hand, and an electric torch in the other, Crane led his companions into Number 12, and played the light as they ascended the stairs.

They were too late. No huddled figure was now lying near the top of the second staircase. Edgar Creed had recovered from his injuries, and taken to flight. He also had vanished into the maze of London, and it would be difficult, if not impossible, to trace him.

It was another disappointment for Crane.

'Everything has gone wrong tonight,' he

declared. 'The tragedy at the Café Spartos, the murder of Leonard Drewitt, the escape of Harrap — and now the disappearance of Edgar Creed! It is most aggravating!'

'There is one consolation,' said Pollard, 'Creed hasn't any idea where to look for Harrap.'

Crane shrugged his shoulders. 'Neither have we,' he replied. 'We have lost track of both men.'

They climbed to the top landing, and entered the front room, which George Harrap occupied. It was in darkness. Crane lit the gas, and saw at a glance that a board had been prised up from the floor.

Beneath it was a shallow space, and in that space the rubies had doubtless been concealed during Harrap's short stay at 12 Pollen Street. But there was no sign of them now.

Crane thoroughly searched the room, however, ransacking every nook and corner of it, removing the mattress from the bed. He found nothing at all, and there was a worried expression on his face

163

when he went downstairs with Yardley and Pollard.

'I am going straight to Scotland Yard, Harry,' he remarked, as they passed out of the house. 'I must have a talk with Inspector Pidgeon, and give him some fresh instructions.'

He bade goodnight to Jim Yardley, who started across the street, then stopped abruptly and turned back.

'I have just remembered something,' he said. 'I wonder I didn't think of it before. I went into the post office round in Regent Street at noon today to buy some stamps, and I saw the man Harrap there.'

'What was he doing?' Crane inquired.

'He was waiting to hand a parcel in at the registry window.'

'A parcel? What was it like?'

'It was a small, square one, the shape of a cardboard box, and it was tied with stout cord and sealed with wax.'

Crane gave a quick start. 'You didn't notice the address, I suppose,' he said.

'I did, as it happens,' Jim Yardley replied. 'I couldn't help seeing it, as I was standing close behind the man. The parcel was addressed to William Marsh, at the central post office at Dover, and it was to be called for. The writing was very legible, and I read it at a glance. Dover was the place. I couldn't be mistaken.'

'You are certain the man was Harrap?'

'I am positive, sir. I saw him go in a moment before I did.'

'Did he see you, Yardley?'

'No, I am sure he didn't. His back was towards me, and he was in the same position when I left.'

A parcel sent registered to Dover! Crane looked at Pollard, a keen sparkle in his eyes.

It was all clear to him. What he had been told was of the greatest importance. That he had been defeated tonight, that he had lost track of Creed and Harrap, was a matter of no consequence now. He would be able to retrieve his defeat.

'I am very glad you gave me this information, Yardley,' he said. 'Harrap has led us and Creed on a false scent. The rubies were in the parcel you saw him post. He sent them to Dover today, meaning to go there for them later, because he feared they might not be safe in his possession, and he was anxious to be rid of them for a time. That is the explanation. He had an appointment at a café in Soho tonight with a man who knew he had the stones, and he suspected that man would try to follow him to his lodgings with a view to robbing him.'

It was a logical deduction.

'There is something else I would like to know,' Crane continued. 'Was the address the only writing on the parcel?'

'No, there was some smaller writing on an upper corner of it,' Jim Yardley replied, 'but I couldn't read it.'

'Ah, that's all right, then!' Crane declared. 'The smaller writing was of course a fictitious name, and a false London address. Harrap will not have any difficulty in getting the parcel.'

He pondered for a moment, and went on, speaking to Pollard.

'You must run down to Dover by an early train in the morning. In all likelihood George Harrap will call at the post office in the course of tomorrow, Harry. He won't delay. Knowing that

Edgar Creed will be searching for him, and that the police will be after him for the murder of Spartos and of Drewitt, he will lose no time in trying to cross to the Continent.'

'And probably by a boat from Dover,' said the young man.

'Yes, I suppose that is why he sent the rubies there.'

'I dare say, Li. By the way, it has just occurred to me that Creed might have got on Harrap's track after Leonard Drewitt was shot. I wonder if he did?'

Crane shook his head.

'I should think not,' he replied. 'The C.I.D. man must have been murdered soon after Harrap escaped from you, and while Creed was still lying stunned on the staircase.

'We will find a taxi now, Harry,' he added, 'and go to Scotland Yard. In the morning I will give you full instructions as to what you're to do in Dover.'

11

A Terrible Discovery

When Pollard arrived at Dover, between nine and ten o'clock the next morning, he went straight to the Central Post Office, in King Street, and inquired for the postmaster.

He gave him a letter written by Lionel Crane, and the postmaster, quite willing to oblige the famous detective, allowed the young man to sit in an inner room, from which he could see everybody who came into the front office.

The instructions he had received from Crane were explicit. In the event of George Harrap calling for the parcel, Pollard was simply to shadow him, and not have him arrested unless he should attempt to cross to the Continent.

Otherwise, should Harrap take a room at some hotel or lodging-house, or should he take a train back to London, the young man was to telegraph to Crane, who would stay at home during the day waiting for a message.

It was not certain that the crook would promptly put in an appearance. He might think it best to let the rubies remain in the care of the post office for some time. That was unlikely, however. It was to be presumed that he meant to get to the other side of the Channel without any delay.

The day wore on. Pollard kept constant vigil, not going out for luncheon; and he was tired and hungry when, at four o'clock in the afternoon, a well-dressed man with a black moustache and side-whiskers, carrying a new suitcase, walked into the office and stepped to the counter.

'I think there is a registered parcel here for me,' he said to a clerk, in a voice that was audible to Pollard. 'It would have been sent from London, and I was to call for it.'

'What name?' asked the clerk.

'Marsh is my name,' was the reply, 'William Marsh.'

'And the name and address of the sender, sir?'

'Robert Lambert, of Number 33 Park Street, Camden Town.'

The clerk nodded. He turned away, and came back shortly with the parcel and a slip of paper.

'You must sign for it,' he said to the man, handing him a pen.

George Harrap — his identity had been clearly established — signed the receipt form, and put the parcel in his suitcase; then left the office, and bore in the direction of the harbour.

Pollard was soon in pursuit of him, and he had gone for some little distance when he noticed, between himself and the crook, a respectable-looking man who wore a soft hat and spectacles, and had a short, grey beard and a drooping moustache.

There was something vaguely familiar about his walk. The young man's suspicions had been roused. He watched the man, and was at length convinced, from his movements, that he was following Harrap.

'The fellow is Edgar Creed,' he murmured. 'I am sure of it. He must have got on to Harrap's track last night, and he has had him under surveillance ever since.'

There could be no doubt, it seemed, that he was right. It was an ominous discovery. Edgar Creed had, of course, seen Harrap get the registered parcel at the post office, and he must suspect what it contained.

When and how would he try to secure the rubies? And what did Harrap mean to do? Was he going to cross to Calais or Boulogne, or to Ostend?

'There is no telling what will happen,' Pollard reflected. 'I shall have to be very much on my guard.'

There were many people on the streets, and that made the game easy. Moreover, it was obvious that neither of the men was suspicious. George Harrap did not once glance behind him, nor did Creed.

Warily shadowed by the young man, who was well disguised, they went along Snargate Street, and past the harbour station, down to the harbour, and out on to the Admiralty Pier.

They stopped near the Lord Warden Hotel, separated by a space of a few yards; and Pollard, lurking in the rear, looked watchfully on. There were a couple of policemen close at hand, he observed, with relief. He would have both of the crooks arrested should they attempt to go on board a boat.

Presently a train arrived, and the passengers swarmed towards a steamer that was lying off the pier, with smoke pouring from its funnels.

It could not be doubted that it was Harrap's intention to cross the Channel.

Otherwise he would not have come here. But he did not approach the vessel. He merely watched it.

He appeared to be in a state of vacillation, and when finally he moved away, retracing his steps in the direction from which he had come, it was evident that he had changed his mind.

'He daren't risk it,' Pollard said to himself. 'He is afraid the police are watching for him, and he will be questioned and searched. He may wait for the night boat. Or perhaps he has concluded to return to London. I hope he will get a room somewhere now, or go to a restaurant. I want to wire to Li.'

George Harrap didn't go to either a hotel or a restaurant, however. He walked up into the town, still shadowed by Edgar Creed, and made his way to the Priory Station. He was going back to London. That was certain.

The booking office was almost deserted.

Harrap took a ticket at the window, and so did Creed; and, a short distance apart from each other, they passed through the gates to the platform, where a train was in readiness.

Pollard had the half of a return-ticket. He waited for a few seconds, then went to the barrier, and spoke to the inspector, handing him his card. The man stared at it in surprise.

'I've heard of you, he said. 'You are Lionel Crane's partner — eh?'

Pollard nodded.

'That's right,' he replied. 'Those two men who passed just now are crooks, and I am shadowing them for Crane. Will you please tell me what tickets they had?'

'First-class singles to Victoria,' was the answer.

'When does the train leave?'

'Not for a quarter of an hour, young man.'

This was satisfactory to Pollard. Having ample time to spare, he went leisurely to the telegraph office, and wrote out a message to Crane. He described the appearance of both Harrap and Creed, and continued as follows:

'We are going to get two birds with one stone. Harrap has the rubies, and I will see he isn't robbed of them on the journey. The train starts in a few minutes. Don't be late in getting to Victoria. You had better take Creed on, and I will shadow Harrap. Or you may decide to arrest them both as soon as they arrive. In any event, we will have to be very careful, though Harrap hasn't any idea that Creed is on his scent, and neither of them had noticed me.'

The telegram despatched, Pollard returned to the platform. He twice paced the length of it, stopping now and again to peer furtively from the shelter of a pillar, but he did not see either of the crooks. Had they taken alarm, and disappeared?

The young man was apprehensive. He climbed on to the train at the rear, and began to search, going from corridor to corridor. In the second carriage, in a first-class compartment, he saw George Harrap. The man was alone. He was stretched comfortably on a seat, with his face towards the window, and his suitcase was in the rack overhead.

Passing on, Pollard entered the next carriage and went through it; and in the one beyond he had a glimpse of Edgar Creed, who was also alone in a first-class compartment. He was smoking a cigar and reading a newspaper.

With an easy mind the young man returned to the carriage he had just left, and settled himself in an empty compartment; and he had hardly more than done so when the guard waved his flag, and the train moved out of the station.

It was a fast express. Folkestone would be the only stop before Victoria was reached, and it was not to be feared that the crooks would get off there. To hide in London again was George Harrap's object.

As Pollard was in the middle carriage, with Creed in the one in front of him and Harrap in the next carriage at the rear, he could make sure that nothing happened to the latter during the run up to town.

'All I've got to do is to keep my eyes open, and watch the corridor,' he reflected. 'Creed can't come through without my seeing him. I don't suppose he has any intention of coming, though. He wouldn't risk murder and robbery on the train. His game is to track Harrap to his lodgings, and rob him there.'

The express stopped for a short interval at Folkestone, and went thundering on its way. Pollard remained on the alert, his gaze never leaving the corridor, while the sunset glow faded and darkness fell.

For some reason — a signal must have been set against it — the train stopped again at a lonely spot in the environs of London; but almost at once it moved on.

Swiftly it threaded the suburbs of the

great city, rumbled across the Thames, and rolled into the vast terminus at Victoria.

Hastening from his compartment, the young man descended from the front end of the carriage, walked forward along the platform, and stopped by the engine. He saw Edgar Creed pass and observed a little beyond him a man with a beard. The man was Lionel Crane in disguise. He raised his arm, and thus disclosed his identity to Pollard.

He had seen the crook. He let him go by and followed and the two disappeared in the crowd.

Crane was on Edgar Creed's trail, but where was George Harrap? Did Creed mean to watch for him at the barrier? Was that why he had pushed ahead of the train?

The young man waited for a short time, looking behind him, scanning the approaching passengers. Harrap was not amongst them. There was no sign of the second crook. What had become of him?

At length, when the platform had nearly emptied, a sickening suspicion flashed to Pollard's mind.

'I am afraid I have lost the fellow,' he said to himself. 'He may have given me the slip by getting off the train on the other side and crossing the line to the opposite platform.'

He walked quickly to the rear, and swung on to the carriage next to the last one; hurried along the corridor and entered the end compartment. One glance, and a cry of horror burst from his lips.

George Harrap had been murdered. He lay there dead, still stretched on the seat, his skull shattered by a heavy blow, a frozen look of agony on his face. He had probably not seen who had struck him as his head was towards the door.

At his feet, where it had been flung by the murderer, was a bar of steel, stained with blood. The suitcase was open on the floor, and the clothes it had contained were scattered about. The registered parcel had gone. It was not in the suitcase, not in the dead man's pockets.

The fatal rubies had cost yet another life. The fifth victim. First the clerk at the mines of Mogok, then John Burnley, then Marc Spartos, then Leonard Drewitt — and now George Harrap, who had himself slain three men, and had been an accomplice with Burnley in the murder of Neil Allison in Burma. The, curse attached to those crimson jewels was still potent. How many more lives would it claim?

Was it Edgar Creed, though, who had murdered Harrap? If so, how had he got here? He had certainly not passed through the middle carriage, and he had not stepped from the express at Folkestone.

Pollard was bewildered at first, and then the explanation occurred to him. It was a very simple one. The moment the train stopped in the environs of London, in the darkness of the night, Creed had descended from his compartment and hastened to the rear; climbed to the carriage next to the last one, and slipped unobserved into the compartment at the farther end of it.

He had promptly killed Harrap, ransacked the suitcase, and found the registered parcel. In the meantime, while he was engaged in the search, the train had started, and was already moving rapidly.

Not daring to jump off, he had coolly entered another carriage — probably the one at the end — and remained there until he got to Victoria, when he had taken to flight with his plunder.

'It is all clear to me now,' Pollard reflected. 'Creed seized his opportunity when the train stopped. He has stolen Harrap's money as well as the rubies, of course. But little does he dream that Mr. Crane is hot on his track. He will be arrested tonight, and — '

A heavy hand clapped the young man on the shoulder. He swung round with a start, and found himself in the grasp of an official of the company, a man in the uniform of an inspector.

12

Baffled Again!

'I've got you, young fellow!' exclaimed the inspector, as he whipped a pistol from his pocket. 'Murder and robbery — eh? Don't move a finger! If you attempt to escape I will put a bullet into you!'

'You've got the wrong party,' Pollard calmly replied. 'I hadn't anything to do with this murder.'

'Oh, hadn't you? The train has been in for five or six minutes. What are you doing here?'

'I have travelled up from Dover. Fetch a policeman, and I will explain to him. You wouldn't believe me if I told you I was Lionel Crane's partner.'

'Not likely, young man!'

'That is who I am, though. I have a card, inspector.'

'A card? It wouldn't prove anything.'

Pollard's shabby appearance was against

him, and the inspector was naturally incredulous. Holding his prisoner tightly with one hand, he threw the door open with the other, and called to a railway constable who was passing by. The man entered the compartment, and stared at the ghastly sight.

'My word, a case of murder!' he gasped.

The inspector nodded gravely.

'Have you seen Mr. Collier anywhere about, Jackson?' he asked.

'Yes, I think you will find him near the Continental booking office,' was the reply. 'I saw him there a bit ago.'

The inspector lowered the window blinds, and, bidding the constable take charge of Pollard, he left the compartment, shut the door behind him, and hastened away.

He returned shortly with a big, blond-moustached man whom Pollard knew well — a Scotland Yard detective, Basil Collier by name, who was frequently on duty at Victoria looking for pickpockets and luggage thieves.

The young man partially removed his

disguise sufficiently to make himself recognisable. Basil Collier scrutinised him closely and laughed.

'You have made a mistake, Farrell,' he said to the inspector. 'This is Lionel Crane's partner without a doubt. I suppose you discovered the murder, Pollard?' he continued. 'What do you know about it?'

'I know a great deal, as it happens,' the young man replied. 'The dead man is no other than George Harrap.'

'George Harrap!' cried the detective. 'The man who was wanted for the murders of John Burnley, Marc Spartos and Leonard Drewitt! Are you sure of that?'

'It is quite right. I have been shadowing Harrap in Dover today, and I travelled back to town on the same train with him this evening.'

'Then you can tell me who murdered him, perhaps.'

'Yes, he was killed and robbed by Edgar Creed, the crook. He was on the train, too. He escaped, but Mr. Crane is on his track, and he won't lose him. There's not much fear of that.'

Pollard briefly related all that had occurred, telling why Crane had sent him down to Dover, and of the events of the day.

'That chief of yours is an uncommonly shrewd man, to give him his due,' declared Basil Collier. 'He has done some clever work in this case. Harrap murdered by Edgar Creed, and Creed has the Burmese rubies! Inspector Pidgeon will be interested. He has been in Mr. Crane's confidence. You had better come to the Yard with me at once, young man, and tell your story there. You can go home afterwards.' He turned to the railway inspector. 'This fellow is beyond suspicion, Farrell,' he said. 'I can vouch for that.'

Pollard would have preferred to go straight home and wait for Crane. He was anxious to know what success he had had. He consented to accompany the detective, however.

They left the compartment, and having with some difficulty squeezed through a crowd that had gathered outside the gates

— the news had spread quickly — they got a taxi and drove to Scotland Yard.

They found Inspector Pidgeon in his room upstairs, and it appeared he had already heard of the sensational crime at Victoria. He had been informed on the telephone by an official of the company.

But he had no knowledge of the affair other than the mere fact that a man had been murdered in a compartment of a train from Dover, and he listened with keen interest to the story Pollard poured into his ears.

'There have been nothing but murders in this case,' he said, when he had learned all. 'John Burnley, the proprietor of the Café Spartos, and Leonard Drewitt. And tonight George Harrap. There can be no doubt, of course, that he was killed by Edgar Creed.'

'Not a bit,' Pollard replied. 'Creed has the rubies, but he won't have them for long. My chief will track him to his lodgings, and then he will go to Welbeck Street to wait for me. I was to meet him there. I will hurry along now, Mr. Pidgeon. It is important that — '

'You had better stay here,' the inspector interrupted. 'Mr. Crane rang me up on the telephone a few minutes ago, just before I heard of the murder, to ask me to be in readiness to assist him tonight, as he expected to make two arrests. He told me he had shadowed Edgar Creed from Victoria to a flat near Charing Cross, and that you were trailing George Harrap, who had the rubies in his possession. He said he was going home to see if you were there, and if you were not, he would wait until you arrived and come on to the Yard with you.'

'He didn't mention the address of the flat?'

'I had no particulars from him, young man. He told me at the last, though, that he was inclined to think Creed might have the rubies.'

'Ah, I can guess why he suspected that! He naturally would. But there is no use in my staying here, Mr. Pidgeon, as the chief will wait for me at home.'

'No, he won't. I will telephone to him.'

Basil Collier departed, remarking that he must return to Victoria. Inspector

Pidgeon turned to the telephone on his desk, and called Lionel Crane's number. He was promptly put through, and after a short conversation he dropped the receiver.

'I have been speaking to his manservant,' he told Pollard. 'Crane has been home and gone, leaving a message for you with Linker. He was to tell you that you would find him at Scotland Yard.'

'That's all right, then,' said Pollard. 'He will soon be here.'

They did not have to wait long. In the course of ten minutes the door was opened and Crane entered the room undisguised. He stared at the young man in surprise.

'You here!' he exclaimed. 'How is this? You could not have had my message! What of George Harrap? I hope you haven't lost him.'

Pollard shook his head.

'He is dead,' he declared.

'Dead? Murdered?'

'Yes, murdered on the train, Li, by Edgar Creed! And Creed has the rubies!'

'I was afraid murder had been done. I

suspected as much from the fact that Creed did not follow Harrap after he left Victoria. That is why I came on to the Yard. I went home first, and as you were not there I concluded not to wait for you. I felt that I ought to have a consultation with Inspector Pidgeon without delay.'

Pollard briefly told his story. He spoke of the events of the day at Dover, and of the circumstances under which George Harrap had been murdered, and Crane then told what he had accomplished.

'Edgar Creed was nervous,' he said. 'He took precautions. But as it was dark, and there was a great deal of traffic, I had no difficulty in following him without rousing his suspicions. He went on foot as far as Grosvenor Gardens, frequently looking back, before he picked up a taxi. I got another one, and shadowed him, by Piccadilly and Coventry Street, to Leicester Square. He left the cab there, walked round to the Charing Cross Road, and entered Cecil Buildings.

'You know it, Harry. A place of fairly inexpensive flats and residential chambers. I am acquainted with Johnson, the hall porter, and he is a man I can trust. I questioned him, and he gave me the information I wanted. Creed has a flat in Cecil Buildings — No. 9 on the second floor. He has been living there in the name of Alfred Scott for some little time, presumably since he disappeared from Langham Street.

'There is a telephone in the porter's room at the rear of the lower hall. I instructed Johnson to keep watch at the front, in case Creed should go out — I did not want to lose track of him for a moment — and telephoned to the Vine Street police station. I asked them to let me have a plainclothes man for a while, and they sent Charles Darch. I gave him a description of Edgar Creed, and told him to watch for him, and follow him if he appeared. I then rang you up, Pidgeon, and afterwards I went home to see if Pollard had arrived.'

'Well, the game is in our own hands,' said the inspector. 'You have handled the case most cleverly, you and your partner, and the end is now in sight. It is certain that Edgar Creed has the rubies.'

'We can take that for granted,' Crane replied.

'We will arrest him tonight, of course.'

'That is what I am here for, Pidgeon.'

'And we will charge him with the murder of George Harrap. There is the strongest kind of evidence against him.'

Crane hesitated.

'We won't charge him with the murder at once,' he said. 'We won't even mention it to him. It might be a mistake to arrest him as soon as we go to his flat.'

'A mistake? The rubies are in Creed's possession. He could not have got rid of them between Victoria and Cecil Buildings,' said Inspector Pidgeon.

'He did not. I know that. Will we find them, though?'

'What do you mean? Are you suggesting that Creed may have swallowed the stones?'

Crane shook his head.

'The flat is rather a large one,' he answered, 'and the rubies are small objects. The flat offers many snug hiding places, and Edgar Creed is a man with a fertile brain. It is possible that he has concealed the rubies so cleverly that we will not be able to discover where they are. That is what I am thinking of. We may be baffled.'

'There is something in that,' the inspector assented.

'And for that reason we must be cautious. But in all likelihood we shall succeed in finding the stones.'

'And if we don't find them, Crane? We won't arrest Creed for the murder of George Harrap?'

'I should prefer not to. No, we had better not arrest him. We will disarm any suspicions he may have, if we can, and have him kept under strict surveillance, by day and night.'

Inspector Pidgeon shrugged his shoulders.

'It is very irregular,' he said. 'I don't like your methods. However, you can have your own way. For my part, I haven't much doubt we shall find the rubies. And now let us be off. We are wasting time.'

'We will go at once,' Crane replied. 'I dare say Creed will be at his flat. He has had a long day of it, and he must be tired.

191

Perhaps he is in bed. He is a desperate man, Pidgeon, and we shall have to be very careful. Should his outer door not be bolted, we will open it quietly with the porter's duplicate key, and slip quietly in. Otherwise we will force the door with a jemmy and rush in.'

'With drawn revolvers,' said Pollard. 'Take it from me, Li, Creed won't be caught napping.'

* * *

While the consultation was going on at Scotland Yard, not very far from the Charing Cross Road, Edgar Creed was seated in the comfortably-furnished sitting room of his flat in Cecil Buildings, by a table on which were a cold supper the porter had brought up to him, a half-bottle of champagne, and a small flagon of choice old brandy.

He was not disguised as he had been during the day. While driving in the cab from Victoria he had removed his spectacles and his grey beard, and substituted a fair, heavy moustache for the false one. And on arriving at the flat he had changed his clothes, though there were no bloodstains on the ones he was wearing.

He felt no remorse, no compunction. He was a callous man, as ruthless as a hungry wolf. From the first he had determined to have the rubies, and tonight, after patient efforts, he had got them by murdering George Harrap.

There was no fear in his guilty heart. He had covered his tracks well, he was sure. He would be suspected, of course. But he was in safe hiding, for one thing; and for another, how could the murder be fastened on him?

He was enjoying himself now, eating and drinking with an easy mind. He was a gourmand, a *bon viveur*, when he had the money to gratify his luxurious tastes. Having finished his supper and the champagne with it, he lit an excellent cigar, leaned back in his chair and sipped the old brandy with a relish.

'I have beaten Lionel Crane at every point,' he reflected, 'and it was worth all the trouble, all the risk. I shall have to lie low for a time, but in the end I will slip over to the Continent, and it will be a long while before England sees me again. It would be more prudent, perhaps, to dispose of the rubies abroad. It would be at a sacrifice, though. I can get a much better price, possibly the full value, if I wait until — '

What was that? Startled by a splintering, crackling noise, the crook sprang to his feet, and reached to his hip pocket for a pistol. But he had no chance to draw it.

The door leading to the hall was thrown open, and Lionel Crane and Inspector Pidgeon dashed into the room, followed by Pollard and Charles Darch. Each had an automatic in his hand.

'Up with your arms!' cried Crane. 'Be quick!'

Edgar Creed obeyed the command. For an instant he was a picture of terror, grey to the lips, and then he pulled himself together. He was calm now; marvellously calm, and cool, and collected, though he had not a doubt that the intrusion meant his arrest on a charge of murdering George Harrap.

'This is a very high-handed proceeding, Mr. Crane,' he said arrogantly. 'I have always been under the impression that a Britisher's home was his castle.'

'It is never a refuge from the law,' Crane replied.

'You have no justification for breaking into my flat.'

'We have every justification.'

'Will you kindly explain, sir?'

'I will tell you in a few words, Creed. We want the rubies.'

Edgar Creed's relief was intense. It appeared, since the murder had not been mentioned, that he was not suspected; or at least that there was no evidence to connect him with the crime. Yet he could not be sure. He was perplexed and uneasy.

'You have made a mistake,' he said. 'Something has put you on a false scent. I haven't got the rubies. I wish I had.'

'You have got them,' Crane answered. 'There is no use in denying it.'

'Not a bit,' declared Inspector Pidgeon. 'You can't fool us, you rascal. We know what we are doing.'

Edgar Creed laughed.

'This is really amusing,' he replied. 'Why come to me, when you are perfectly aware of the fact that the rubies have been in George Harrap's possession since last night? I haven't the slightest idea where he is, or I might have tried to rob him, to be candid.'

'You have not seen Harrap during the day?' Crane asked.

'I have not. I haven't even been looking for him. But I think I understand. Harrap has been arrested. The rubies were not on him, and you jumped to the conclusion that I had them.'

'There is good reason to believe that you have, Creed.'

'What reason, sir?'

'On the ground of strong suspicions.'

'Suspicions? Is that all?'

Edgar Creed was readily deceived. It was quite clear now, he felt, that Lionel Crane and his companions had not even heard of the train murder.

'You have made a mistake,' he repeated. 'However, you had better search the place.'

'We intend to,' said Crane.

'I wish you to. You will have your trouble for nothing, though.'

'Possibly. Probably not. We may have to do some damage, Creed, and for that I will be personally responsible.'

Edgar Creed was searched first. The rubies were not on him. They were not concealed in his clothing, in his boots, anywhere on his body. Bank notes to the value of nearly three hundred pounds were in one of his pockets, but Crane replaced the money, making no remark about it.

The sitting room was searched next, and in the most thorough manner. Instructed by Crane, Inspector Pidgeon and Pollard, and Charles Darch, scoured cabinets and drawers, and looked into vases and bottles; ripped off the leather upholstery of chairs and a couch, and shifted rugs and the carpet; examined the floor boards — there was no hollow space between them — and sounded the panelled walls; dragged down the draperies that hung at the windows, and felt under the steam radiator. The rubies were not found. They were certainly not in the sitting room.

Leaving Charles Darch there to guard

Creed, the others went over the whole of the premises, and searched as thoroughly as they had searched before.

They scoured the hall, then the bathroom, and finally the bedchamber, where they moved the carpet, and tapped the walls; mutilated chairs, and made sure that the bedposts were not hollow; ransacked a wardrobe, and a chest of drawers; turned the mattress on the bed over, and ripped it apart.

Still the rubies were not discovered. Two hours had been spent in the fruitless task, and there was nowhere else to search now.

Not yet satisfied, Crane opened every window of every room, gazed above him, and felt the walls below to see if there were any loose bricks. He finished with the sitting room, and now he was absolutely convinced, beyond the shadow of a doubt, that the rubies were not anywhere in the flat.

Where could they be? What had the crook done with them? It was certain that he had stolen them from George Harrap, and equally certain that they had been in his possession when he arrived at Cecil Buildings.

He had not slipped out while the porter was watching the entrance and Crane was using the telephone, or while Charles Darch was mounting guard in the street; and there was no exit from the building at the rear. It was a baffling mystery.

During the conduct of the search Edgar Creed had been sitting quietly in a chair, sipping his brandy, smoking cigar after cigar, and chatting amiably with Charles Darch. There was a mocking smile on his face. 'It is a pity you have wasted your time, Mr. Crane,' he said. 'It must be a great disappointment to you. To imagine that I had the rubies! It was stupid of you to get such a delusion into your head.'

It was with difficulty that Crane kept his temper.

'It appears that I was mistaken,' he coldly replied. 'I owe you an apology.'

'I accept it, sir. I have no ill-feeling. By the way, there will be a heavy bill for damages.'

'I will pay it. You need not worry about that.'

There was no more to be said, nothing more to be done. Crane went downstairs with his companions, and questioned the hall-porter.

'Could Mr. Scott have got into any of the other flats on his floor?' he inquired.

'Impossible, sir,' the man answered. 'His key would not have opened any of the other doors.'

'Were any of the occupants of the flats on that floor in when I first came here, and during the next hour?'

'All of them were, sir, and they have been in ever since.'

It was obvious, from the porter's statements, that Edgar Creed could not have concealed the rubies in somebody else's flat. That theory must be abandoned.

The little party left the building, chagrined and mystified, irritated by their defeat. Charles Darch remained outside to keep watch, and the others walked slowly down the Charing Cross Road.

'The cunning rogue!' said Inspector Pidgeon. 'He has tricked us neatly. We ought to have arrested him on the murder charge.'

'Had we taken him into custody,' Crane replied, 'in all likelihood we should never have found the rubies?'

'You think you will find them eventually?'

'Yes, sooner or later. It is a question of time.'

'You believe they are somewhere in the flat, Crane?'

'I do not. I have no idea where they can be. I am sure they are in the building, though.'

'Well, what is to be done next?' asked the inspector.

'What I told you before,' said Crane. 'Edgar Creed must be watched incessantly, followed wherever he goes, from morning till night, from night till morning. I will leave that to Pollard, and to one of your men from the Yard. They will take turns at it. I will keep out of the way, and I shall take steps to deceive Creed, to put him under the impression that he is not being shadowed.

'Come home with me, Pidgeon,' he added, as he stopped a taxi, 'and we will have a talk there.'

13

Shadowing the Crook

On the afternoon of the following day there appeared in several of the London evening papers two paragraphs which Crane had inserted with a view to deceiving Edgar Creed, though he doubted if he would accomplish his object.

One of the paragraphs, relating to the tragedy at Victoria, stated that the police had no clue whatever to the identity of the murderer, and were not likely to get one. And the other paragraph was to the effect that Lionel Crane, it was learned, had dropped what work he was engaged on, and had gone north at the earnest request of a Scottish millionaire, at whose castle in the Western Highlands certain mysterious and inexplicable events of a most sinister nature had recently occurred.

'Creed knows, of course, that I am positive it was he who murdered George

Harrap,' Crane said to Pollard, after the paragraphs appeared, 'and knowing also that I believe he stole the rubies from Harrap, he will presumably conclude that I have kept my knowledge from the police with the intention of handling the case alone, and with the primary object of recovering the jewels. If he does so conclude it will be more to my advantage than otherwise. He will not be afraid that Scotland Yard men are assisting me.

'As for the other paragraph in the papers, Creed may shrewdly judge that it is a blind, meant to put him off his guard. But if he should credit it, be deluded into the belief that I am in Scotland, he will probably attempt to get abroad with the rubies, or to dispose of them in London. And on that I am building my hopes.'

Never was espionage more thoroughly conducted than in this instance; never with more care and pains. Not for a moment was Edgar Creed free from it except when he was in his flat.

For a week, by day and night, he was patiently, warily, adroitly shadowed, kept under constant surveillance, by Pollard, and by a Scotland Yard man of the name of Hawke. They relieved each other, and they frequently changed their disguises.

Nothing came of it, however. Their skill was wasted. The crook did not play into their hands during that week.

Expensively dressed, in the height of fashion, he devoted himself to the sheer joy of living, and freely spent the money he had stolen from George Harrap.

He strolled in the Park, and wandered about the West End, making purchases at shops in Bond Street and Piccadilly. He sat in luxurious cafés, and lunched and dined at the best restaurants, where he drank wines of the rarest vintage, and smoked the choicest brands of cigars. And every night he went either to a theatre or a music hall, and had supper afterwards.

Always he was alone. He never spoke to a friend or acquaintance. He pursued his own way, and, meanwhile, he had waxed and twisted his fair moustache as before, and let the tuft of beard on his chin grow.

Did he know he was being watched? In all likelihood he did not, so shrewdly was it done. If he was aware of the fact, though, he made no effort to elude his shadowers. It might be that he hoped to wear out their patience, and convince them that he had no knowledge of the rubies.

Thus the week dragged fruitlessly by, and then, at eleven o'clock one morning, something happened — something that was to have far-reaching results.

The Scotland Yard sleuth was off duty, and Pollard was sitting in a little dairy shop on the west side of the Charing Cross Road, with a sandwich and a glass of milk, when he saw an empty taxi stop in front of Cecil Buildings. And a moment later Edgar Creed came out to the street, stepped into the cab, and was driven in the direction of Charing Cross.

It was quick work. The startled fellow looked for another taxi, and, seeing none in sight, he hurried across to the building, and questioned the hall-porter.

'That cab Mr. Scott has gone off in must have been sent for,' he said. 'Did you get it for him?'

'No, sir,' replied the porter, who was in Lionel Crane's pay. 'The gentleman must have sent for it himself. There is a telephone in his flat.'

'Did you hear what he said to the chauffeur, Johnson?'

'I did, as it happens. Mr. Scott spoke very low, but I was listening, and I caught the words. He told the chauffeur to go to Waterloo Station.'

Pollard hastened away. He picked up a taxi by the rear entrance to the Alhambra, bidding the driver go by Wellington Street and the river to the Waterloo Bridge Road; and during the ride he bent his mind on the unexpected move the crook had made.

It was a significant one. For one thing, Edgar Creed had left his flat much earlier than usual. For another, he had on previous occasions invariably walked to some West End café for an aperitif. Why, then, this break from the routine of his daily life? What was his intention now? Had he the rubies with him, and did he mean to travel to Southampton, and sail for some foreign country?

No, that was highly improbable. This morning, as heretofore, he was not disguised, and he was too lightly attired for a sea-trip in such chilly weather. Furthermore, he had no luggage. He had taken no bag with him, not even an overcoat.

Yet, on the other hand, he had ordered a taxi by telephone, and it must have been for the purpose of shaking off pursuit. He had been aware from the first that his movements were under surveillance.

'There can be only one explanation,' Pollard reflected. 'He is going to Waterloo to meet somebody. And through that person, I dare say, I shall get on the trail of the rubies.'

Having reached the big terminus of the Southern Railway, the young man mounted the steps, and sauntered carelessly, on chance, towards the arrival platform of the main line. Edgar Creed was there, standing near the barrier. Pollard stood within several yards of him, and waited.

A quarter of an hour elapsed, and at length a notice board was displayed. It stated that a boat train from Plymouth was due, and shortly afterwards the train rolled into the station.

'Somebody from America?' murmured Pollard. 'That's damned queer. I may be wrong, though.'

The gates were opened, and amidst noise and confusion the passengers streamed along the platform in a jostling throng. From their un-English clothing, and the nasal twang of their voices, it was obvious that the greater part of them were Americans.

As they passed through the gates they brushed by Edgar Creed. He scanned them closely, and Pollard, from his position, could see both Creed and the passengers without turning his head.

He was very curious to learn who the crook was waiting for. He made several guesses, and guessed wrong every time. The tide flowed on, moving amongst trucks heaped with luggage, and presently there was a break. Edgar Creed waited, his gaze bent on more passengers who were approaching. The foremost of them was a lean, spare man of average height, perhaps fifty years of age, with keen eyes, a scrubby little moustache clipped short, and a dyspeptic complexion. Though he wore a suit of grey serge that was badly cut, and a grey soft hat that was a trifle soiled, there was an air of opulence about him.

He was not alone. He was followed by a black man, who was possibly his valet, and the man carried a suitcase, on which was painted in white letters, 'Cyrus B. Comstock.'

'I believe that is the man Creed is looking for,' Pollard said to himself, as he saw the crook make a sudden move.

He was right this time. The gentleman in grey drew near, and as he came by the barrier Edgar Creed stepped up to him, and said in a voice that was audible to the young man: 'Good morning, Mr. Comstock!'

The American glanced at him sharply.

'Your name?' he inquired.

'Bradlaw,' was the answer. 'Morton Bradlaw.'

'Pleased to meet you. I will have a talk with you later. I am going to the Hotel Majestic. Call on me there in an hour from now.'

'Very well, sir. In an hour.'

The American passed on with his servant. The last of the passengers appeared from the gates, and behind them came a porter drawing a truck that was loaded with big trunks, several of which bore the name of Cyrus B. Comstock.

Looking very well pleased with himself, Edgar Creed strolled to the bar, and sat down at a table. He remained there for the better part of an hour, drinking whisky-and-soda and smoking a cigar. When finally he left the station, and got into a taxi in the York Road, Pollard followed him in another.

The young man had made an important discovery, and there could be little or no doubt, he felt, that it would not be long before the stolen rubies were recovered.

'The name of Cyrus B. Comstock sounds familiar to me,' he reflected. 'I am sure I have read something about him. I can't remember what it was, though.'

14

Edgar Creed Keeps the Appointment

The Hotel Majestic, noted the world over for its exclusiveness, celebrated for its chef, patronised by emperors, kings, and princes — and by millionaires with or without a streak of blue in their blood — was situated in Brook Street, close to Grosvenor Square.

The arrival of Mr. Cyrus B. Comstock at this aristocratic hostelry created quite a commotion. He was expected. He had cabled from New York before sailing for Europe. He had stayed here on previous occasions, and his rooms, the most expensive suite in the building, were ready for him. From Monsieur Escargot, the manager, he had an expansive smile, a profound bow, and an obsequious clasp of the hand. The clerk at the desk absent-mindedly thrust his pen into a bottle of paste, and bent so low that his chin nearly touched his heels. The reception clerk turned his back on a grand duchess to whom he was speaking at the moment.

The pageboy, reminiscent of fabulous tips in the past, stood to attention, and grinned from ear to ear. And an elderly lady from Mushkosh, Missouri, blazing with diamonds, remarked to her husband that the new arrival must be a royal personage.

To all this flattery Cyrus B. Comstock was supremely indifferent.

'Cut out the kowtow stuff, Escargot,' he said dryly. 'I'm a plain American citizen, and darned proud of it, too. I want a bottle of dry Cliquot, and a box of the best Rothschilds. And when a gentleman of the name of Bradlaw calls to see me send him up toot sweet.'

A sumptuous lift shot the honoured guest to his gorgeously furnished apartments on the first floor. Jupiter, the black valet, unpacked the suitcase, and withdrew to wait for the delivery of the heavy luggage.

Cyrus B. Comstock had a bath, and

changed his clothes, and he was settled comfortably in a big Louis Quatorze chair by a table that had belonged to Madame Pompadour, sipping his Veuve Cliquot, feasting his uncultured eyes on a Gobelin tapestry depicting men in green and yellow garments chasing a purple stag, with biscuit-coloured hounds, and enjoying a dry smoke — he was chewing an unlighted cigar — when Mr. Morton Bradlaw was ushered into the room.

'Sit down,' bade Mr. Comstock.

'Thank you,' said Mr. Bradlaw, sinking gracefully into another Louis Quartorze chair.

'Have a drink and a smoke?' asked Mr. Comstock.

'With pleasure,' Mr. Bradlaw assented.

He accepted a glass of champagne, and put a match to an expensive Rothschild. There was a short silence. Cyrus B. Comstock was taking stock of his visitor, whom he had never seen before.

'I had your letter,' he said at length. 'How did you know I was coming to England?'

'It was in a New York paper,' Morton Bradlaw replied.

'And you knew when I would get to Waterloo?'

'I saw in a London paper that the *Carmania* had reached Plymouth late last night, and the boat train would leave at six o'clock this morning.'

'How did you recognise me, Mr. Bradlaw?'

'I have seen an American film of topical events showing you entertaining the Queen of Ruritania at your Fifth Avenue mansion.'

'Ah, yes, I recall it.'

There was a short silence again.

'You stated in your letter,' said Mr. Comstock, 'that you had a number of rare and valuable gems to dispose of.'

'That is so,' Morton Bradlaw answered.

'What are they, sir?'

'They are rubies. I have forty-eight of them, of large size, and of the purest pigeon-blood colour. There are none anywhere to compare with them.'

'I am rather partial to rubies. You can satisfactorily account for their being in your possession, I suppose.'

Morton Bradlaw reflected for a moment.

Under the circumstances he dare not lie, and on the other hand he feared that if he told the truth the American would refuse to bargain with him. He felt he must chance that, however.

'You have doubtless heard of the stones,' he said. 'They were stolen from the mines of Mogok, in Upper Burma, some months ago.'

Cyrus B. Comstock stared in blank stupefaction.

'The mines of Mogok!' he cried. 'Murder and robbery were done there! And you coolly tell me you have those rubies!'

'I have had them for a week or so. That is all.'

'You are not one of the thieves, sir?'

'Most certainly not. I strongly resent your insinuation.'

'I don't know what to believe, Mr. Bradlaw. I have read a great deal about the stones. They are stained with blood. And you propose to sell them to me. I should be afraid to touch them. I ought to inform the police.'

'You won't do that, I am sure.'

'Why not, you rascal?'

'Because you would lose the opportunity of acquiring the finest jewels of their kind in the world.'

'If you think I am unscrupulous enough to buy stolen goods you are very much mistaken,' declared Mr. Comstock.

Morton Bradlaw shrugged his shoulders.

'Would it be the first time you have done so?' he asked.

Mr. Comstock flushed.

'Be careful, sir!' he exclaimed. 'Don't insult me! I am not a rogue like yourself! You could not have come by the rubies honestly. How did you get them?'

'To be perfectly candid,' said Morton Bradlaw, 'I stole them from the man who brought them from Burma to England.'

'You are not ashamed to own up to it?'

'I have told you the truth, Mr. Comstock, because it is best you should know. I have simply robbed a thief. What if I have? It has been rumoured that the source from which you obtained some of the jewels in your collection is open to suspicion.'

Mr. Comstock flushed again.

'There is no foundation for such a rumour,' he said angrily. 'Let me have no more of your insolence. As for the rubies, I decline to bargain with you. Take them to another market.'

'You will change your mind when you have seen them,' urged Morton Bradlaw. 'They are marvellous stones.'

'So I have heard, sir. I don't doubt it.'

'They are superb, unique. Each of them is as large as a filbert.'

'Ah, indeed? And of pure pigeon-blood colour, you say?'

'Absolutely. They are wonderful beyond words. No queen has any to compare with them. It would be quite safe for you to purchase them, for I understand that no one except yourself ever sees your collection.'

'Yes, that is true. But — '

Cyrus B. Comstock broke off, shaking his head. He flung aside the cigar he was chewing, and took another from the box. He hesitated, swayed in two directions. He was struggling between cupidity, intense desire, and what little scruples he possessed. It was not a very hard struggle, though. The cupidity prevailed.

'Where are the rubies?' he inquired. 'Have you got them with you?'

'I have not,' Morton Bradlaw replied.

'They are at your lodgings?'

'No; they are in a much safer place. I can fetch them in an hour.'

'No, no; I haven't decided yet,' said Mr. Comstock. 'It is the risk I am thinking of. I read in a New York paper, the day before I sailed, that the police knew the rubies were in London, and were trying hard to find them. And that they were assisted by Lionel Crane, your London sleuth.'

'They have been searching for months,' Morton Bradlaw answered, 'and what has come of it? Nothing. Crane has done most of the work on the case, and I have beaten him at every point, clever as he is.'

'You have beaten him, sir? What do you mean?'

'I fooled him. He even went so far as to search my flat, in the full belief that — '

Mr. Bradlaw paused abruptly. He had made a slip of the tongue. His face showed a trace of confusion, and Cyrus

B. Comstock was quick to observe it.

'You have said more than you meant to,' he declared. 'So Lionel Crane suspects that you have the rubies!'

'He did suspect it,' Morton Bradlaw replied. 'He doesn't now. He has been completely deceived.'

'He hasn't been watching you since he made the futile search?'

'He couldn't have been. He is in Scotland, working on another case.'

'There are the police to be reckoned with. Have they been keeping you under surveillance? Don't lie to me!'

'I have been shadowed on several occasions, I believe. I am not sure.'

'It is very likely, then,' said Mr. Comstock, 'that you were shadowed to Waterloo this morning.'

'It is impossible,' Morton Bradlaw asserted. 'I took precautions. I telephoned from my flat in the Charing Cross Road to a garage, and had a taxi sent round. As soon as it arrived I drove off, and I can swear that nobody followed me.'

'You looked back?'

'Yes, frequently. And when my taxi

turned into Chandos Street there wasn't another one in sight behind me.'

Cyrus B. Comstock was inclined to be apprehensive. He rose from his chair, and paced to and fro, his brows knit. He stepped to a window, and glanced into Brook Street; sat down again, and started to chew a fresh cigar.

'I don't like it,' he said. 'Lionel Crane still suspects you, I guess. He is a pretty cute detective, and your police are as smart as they make them. I'm not taking any chances of getting into trouble. If I deal with you it will be on conditions. For one thing, you must keep away from your flat for a while.'

'I had no intention of returning,' Morton Bradlaw answered. 'Not until I had disposed of the rubies. Can't we strike a bargain today?'

'No, sir, not today."

'Very well. I will find lodgings somewhere.'

'And you must lie low for twenty-four hours, and disguise yourself.'

'I will do that, Mr. Comstock. And when am I to see you again? When the twenty-four hours have expired?'

Mr. Comstock considered. 'I'll fix things,' he said, after a brief pause. 'I won't negotiate anywhere in London. It might not be safe. I am going down to a lonely part of the country tomorrow for my health and for the trout fishing, and you will follow. You can't come with me. I won't be seen with you at all in public. I shall go in a hired car, and my black servant will drive it. Call here at three o'clock tomorrow afternoon with the rubies in your possession. A letter will be waiting for you in the name of Hammond, and that letter will give you full instructions. Meanwhile, obey my orders. Disguise your features, and avoid your flat. And, by the way, how much are you asking for the stones?'

'One hundred thousand pounds,' replied Morton Bradlaw, who judged it would be useless to demand a larger sum.

'That is rather exorbitant, sir.'

'Exorbitant? They are worth nearly two hundred thousand pounds.'

'Yes, in the open market, perhaps,' Cyrus B. Comstock assented. 'But I am not a dealer in gems. I collect them. Furthermore, I must allow for the risk in purchasing from you. I dare say I shall accept your price, however.

'You will have to excuse me now,' he added. 'It is time for my luncheon, and during the rest of the day I shall be very busy dictating letters to a stenographer. Good morning, Mr. Bradlaw. Three o'clock tomorrow afternoon.'

Thus dismissed, Morton Bradlaw descended the stairs, and passed out to Brook Street. He stopped on the pavement for a moment, while he decided what he would do; and then, followed by Pollard, he bent his steps eastward.

He was in no hurry. He did not take a cab. At a leisurely pace he went to Wardour Street, where he entered the shop of Barkson, the theatrical costumier.

Here he bought a brown beard and a moustache — the young man observed the purchase from without — and when he reappeared, undisguised, he walked round by Leicester Square to the Strand, and thence to Maiden Lane.

His destination was Bonner's Private

Hotel, a modest place patronised by actors. He engaged a room, and went upstairs; and Pollard, who had seen all through the open doorway, and knew he had time to spare, hastened to a chemist's shop in the vicinity, and got on to Scotland Yard on the telephone.

He had a short talk with Inspector Pidgeon, and returned to a point near the hotel; and in a quarter of an hour he was joined by a plainclothes man whom the inspector had sent from the Yard.

Pollard explained matters to him, and gave him instructions; then drove home in a taxi, and related all the events of the morning to Lionel Crane.

'Who is Cyrus B. Comstock, Li?' he continued. 'The name sounds familiar to me. Can you recall him?'

'Yes, I have a clear recollection of him,' Crane replied. 'The American and London papers were full of him a couple of years ago in connection with the famous Orloff sapphire, as it was called. It was of fabulous value, belonging to the Tsar, and it mysteriously disappeared from the Winter Palace at Petrograd, and was next heard of in New York. I cut several clippings from the papers at the time, I remember, and pasted them in one of my — '

Crane broke off, and going to a cabinet, he scanned a row of bulky scrapbooks. He took one of them from the shelf, and with the aid of the index he promptly found what he wanted.

'Ah, here we are!' he said. And he went on, speaking at intervals as he cast his eyes over the columns of printed matter. 'Cyrus B. Comstock, a multi-millionaire of New York. A palatial residence in Fifth Avenue, and a huge country place built in imitation of a German schloss, on the Hudson River. A man of vast wealth, with shares in silver and copper mines, iron mills, motorcar industries, and various others pouring a steady stream of gold into his coffers. His favourite hobby is collecting rare jewels. He has a craze for them, and he will pay any price to get what he sets his heart on. His collection, which he seldom or never shows to even his intimate friends, is in a room in his Fifth Avenue residence — a room with a steel door fitted with a combination lock, and steel walls covered with Gobelin tapestries.'

'Ah, so that's the gentleman from America!' murmured Pollard. 'A millionaire jewel collector!'

'And an unscrupulous one, I imagine,' Crane resumed, reading on. 'It appears that the police, having learned that the Orloff sapphire had found its way to New York, suspected that it was in the possession of Mr. Comstock. They taxed him with buying it, and he gave it up, declaring he had purchased it honestly under a misapprehension. But it was broadly hinted that he was well aware of the fact that it was the Tsar's lost sapphire, and that he would not have admitted that he had it had he not been afraid of getting into serious trouble.'

'Well, Li, I have made an important discovery,' said the young man. 'It is perfectly clear how things stand, isn't it?'

'As plain as a pikestaff, Harry,' Crane answered, rubbing his hands in delight. 'Edgar Creed, and the other two crooks, would have known all about Cyrus B.

Comstock and his collection. It is not likely, though, that Harrap or Burnley had any plans in regard to him. As for Creed, it was only a week ago that he stole the rubies, and therefore he could not have communicated with Mr. Comstock in New York. What he presumably did is this. Having read in a London paper that the millionaire had sailed for England on the *Carmania*, he wrote to him, and marked on the letter that it was to be delivered on the arrival of the boat at Plymouth.'

'That's right, Li. That he did write to him is obvious from the short conversation I overheard between the two men. Each was expecting the other.'

Crane nodded. 'Yes, and Creed subsequently ascertained at what time the boat-train would arrive at Waterloo this morning,' he said, 'and went there to meet Mr. Comstock.'

'With the intention of selling the rubies to him,' declared Pollard.

'Of course. That goes without saying. The game is in our own hands. Cyrus B. Comstock is staying at the Hotel

Majestic, and Laban. Creed is at Bonner's Hotel.'

'And what of the rubies, Li? Do you suppose Creed has them on him?'

'He may have. But I doubt it. We won't arrest him at present. I fear it would be a mistake. On the other hand, I don't believe that Mr. Comstock has the stones. If Creed had already disposed of them, and been paid his price, he would have returned to his flat in the Charing Cross Road, instead of taking a room at the hotel in Maiden Lane. And he would not have bought a false beard and moustache.'

'Yes, that's sound argument. It looks as if Creed either has the rubies with him, or they are still where he concealed them that night. They can't be in Mr. Comstock's possession yet, at all events. Whatever Creed may have told him, he must at least suspect that they are the jewels which were stolen from the Mines of Mogok. I wonder if he will be willing to purchase them?'

'I don't suppose he will have any scruples about it. The temptation will be too strong for him.'

'What beats me,' Pollard continued, 'is where the rubies were hidden when we searched the flat. What on earth could Edgar Creed have done with them? We know that he wasn't outside of the building.'

Crane shrugged his shoulders. 'There is no use in puzzling over that now,' he replied. 'Why should we? We are very close to success. The end of our task is in sight. But we must give both Creed and Cyrus B. Comstock plenty of rope. You and Davis, the man Inspector Pidgeon sent you from the Yard, will watch Edgar Creed alternately. And I will see that Hawke watches the Hotel Majestic, and keeps track of Mr. Comstock's movements. As for myself, I shall simply wait for a development. I had better not take a hand in the game.'

15

Pollard on the Scent

It was Pollard who was on duty, not the Scotland Yard man, when Edgar Creed left Bonner's Hotel at one o'clock on the afternoon of the next day. He was not disguised, but there was nothing significant in that. He could not well alter his appearance while he was staying at the hotel.

He had been out to dinner on the previous night, and on this occasion he went to a well-known restaurant in Maiden Lane. He had a hearty luncheon here, and, leaving the place at one o'clock, he bent his steps to the Strand, and had a drink at a bar; walked slowly to Charing Cross Station, and entered the cloakroom. Furtively watched by Pollard, he handed a slip of paper to the attendant, and received a brown kitbag. He unlocked and opened the bag on the spot, took a light overcoat from it — the weather had turned cold since yesterday — and put it on; locked the bag again, and slipped the key into his pocket.

A few moments later he was spinning westward in a taxi, and Pollard, in another one, was puzzling his brains over a very complex problem.

Had the bag been deposited at the cloakroom before or after the murder of George Harrap? If before, then the rubies could not be inside of it. On the other hand, if it had been deposited after the crime, it presumably contained the rubies.

But how, in that event, had Edgar Creed got to Charing Cross with the bag? He had been followed by Lionel Crane as he drove from Victoria to Cecil Buildings on the night of the train murder. While he was in his flat, prior to its being searched, somebody had been watching out in the street, and the hall porter had been watching from within, and both had been positive that the crook had not left the building.

Moreover, since that night he had been

under constant surveillance except for one short interval. He had eluded the young man when he went from Cecil Buildings to Waterloo, yet he had certainly not had the bag with him then.

'I don't know what the deuce to make of it,' Pollard reflected. 'If the rubies are in the bag, how on earth did they get there, and if they are not in it why is Creed taking the bag to the Hotel Majestic? It is a pretty problem, and one the chief couldn't solve. I'll have to give it up. It is too deep for me.'

The chauffeur, who must have been so instructed by Creed, took a roundabout route. He drove by Westminster and Victoria Street to the Buckingham Palace Road, up Grosvenor Gardens to Hyde Park Corner, and thence direct to the Hotel Majestic.

Pollard was perplexed and uneasy. He feared the crook suspected he was shadowed, and had been trying to verify his suspicions. Such was not the case, however. Edgar Creed had been merely killing time, and it was exactly three o'clock when he stepped from his cab in

Brook Street. He paid the chauffeur, and, disguised by the brown beard and moustache he had purchased on the previous day — he had put them on in the taxi — he entered the hotel, carrying his bag.

Pollard, who was wearing a blue-belted jacket and a cap similar to those worn by District Messenger boys, loitered behind for a few moments, and then approached a constable who was standing on the pavement in such a position that he could see across the hotel courtyard and into the lounge.

He was not a real constable. The man was Larry Hawke, and he had chosen this disguise because, should the crook be suspicious, he would take it for granted that no ordinary policeman could be watching for him.

'I am Pollard,' said the young man, in a low voice, 'and that was Edgar Creed who just passed in.'

'I thought so,' Larry Hawke replied. 'I saw him go straight to the desk. He spoke to the clerk, and the clerk gave him a letter.'

'A letter — eh? What is Creed doing now? I don't want to look.'

'He is sitting on a couch reading the letter.'

'Do you see anything of Mr. Cyrus Comstock? Isn't he there?'

'No, and he won't be. He is gone. He started off two or three hours ago, in a car that was driven by his black servant.'

'In which direction, Hawke?' asked Pollard.

'Towards Grosvenor Square,' the detective answered.

'Did he have any luggage with him?'

'Yes, two kitbags.'

Pollard was quick to understand.

'I'll bet I know the game,' he declared. 'Mr. Comstock is going to buy the rubies, but he is afraid to deal with the crook in London. He has gone out of town, probably to some quiet place in the country. And he left a letter of instruction for Edgar Creed, telling him where to go.'

Continuing, the young man told briefly of Creed's movements, and of the bag he had got at the cloakroom at Charing Cross.

'Ah, then the rubies must have been in that bag,' said Larry Hawke.

'That's what I thought, though I couldn't account for their getting there,' Pollard replied. 'But I'm not so sure now. There are clothes in the bag. Creed may have deposited it there before he murdered George Harrap, and he got it today because he was expecting to go on a journey.'

'He wouldn't join Mr. Comstock unless he had the rubies with him, I should think.'

'He may have them, Hawke. Or perhaps Mr. Comstock has them. Perhaps Creed gave them to him yesterday, and he is to be paid his price today.'

'Very likely. It might be a mistake, then, if we were to arrest Creed?'

'Exactly. We daren't chance that. I will keep track of the fellow. I shan't lose him. There are four or five cabs on the rank yonder, and — '

'He is coming now,' Larry Hawke whispered.

'Right-ho!' said Pollard. 'I will take him on. You go to Welbeck Street, and tell my

234

chief how things have turned out. And tell him also he can expect a telegram from me.'

Edgar Creed had just reappeared from the hotel, still carrying his bag. Throwing a careless glance at the disguised detective and the youth, he walked over to the cab-rank and got into a closed taxi.

The cab glided to Grosvenor Square, and disappeared round the corner to the north, and a few seconds later Pollard was in pursuit in another taxi.

He had given instructions to his chauffeur, and as the chase began he pulled off his jacket, changed the colour of it by turning it inside out, and got into it again; then tossed his blue cap under the seat, and put on a cap of grey tweed which he had in his pocket.

Several deft touches of greasepaint to his face with the aid of a small mirror, and the deception was complete.

'I look a different person now,' he said to himself. 'There's no fear of Creed suspecting I am the District Messenger boy he noticed when he came out of the hotel.'

Separated by a space of a dozen yards or so, and with a couple of other cabs always between them — Pollard's chauffeur shrewdly contrived that — the two taxis raced on, threading the traffic, held up by a constable more than once, and both of them at the same time.

The pursuit led by Oxford Street, the Marble Arch and the Edgware Road, and finally by Praed Street to Paddington Station. And now it was quite clear that Edgar Creed was going to keep an appointment with Cyrus B. Comstock somewhere in the West Country.

He was not suspicious. He did not look behind him. He went to the booking office, and Pollard, following closely, heard him say to the clerk:

'I want a first-class ticket to Countisbury.'

'There is no such station on our line,' the clerk told him.

'I made a mistake,' was the reply. 'I meant Lynmouth.'

It was fortunate the young man had overheard the conversation. It might save him some trouble. Countisbury, he knew well, was a tiny place little more than a mile from Lynmouth.

It was there obviously that the crook and the millionaire were to meet. And Edgar Creed was not returning to London by rail. He was to come back in the car with Mr. Comstock. Pollard took a ticket to Lynmouth, and when he had seen the crook get into a compartment of a train that was in readiness, and had ascertained that he had ten minutes to spare, he hastened to the telegraph office and wrote out a message that ran thus:

'Lionel Crane, Welbeck Street, London. Mr. Comstock has gone to Lynmouth in a car and Creed is going by rail. I am travelling with him. Come as quickly as you can. You had better bring Inspector Pidgeon along.'

Pollard handed the message in, and returned to the platform. He got into a first-class compartment, and shortly afterwards the train started.

16

A Signal of Danger

Travelling by way of Barnstaple, and changing there to the narrow gauge railway, Edgar Creed and Pollard arrived at Lynton, the end of the line, shortly after nine o'clock at night.

They had a mile farther to go, and, finding a small motor-bus waiting at the station, they got into it with other passengers, and were driven down to the charming village of Lynmouth, on the Bristol Channel.

Pollard kept a wary eye on the crook's movements. It was evident that Creed was not to be met here by Mr. Comstock, for without any hesitation he crossed the bridge spanning the East Lyn, and disappeared around the spur of a hill, holding to the steep road that ascended for a mile or, so to the tiny hamlet of Countisbury.

'That is where the deal is to be,' the young man said to himself. 'In that secluded little village. The two of them intend to spend the night there, of course, so I needn't be uneasy. The chief will be coming along presently. I can expect him in a couple of hours.'

It was too late for dinner, so Pollard entered the bar of the Lyndale Hotel and called for a sandwich and a glass of beer. He consumed them quickly, and then went from the bar to the front porch of the building.

And he had been sitting there for less than an hour, watching for his partner, when a big car came chugging down the road that wound up through the deep valley of the East Lyn to Watersmeet, and stopped close to the hotel.

The young man recognised it at once, and hastened to it. Lionel Crane was in the car, and with him was Inspector Pidgeon.

'I thought I should find you here,' said Crane. 'You didn't expect me so soon, I suppose.'

'Not for another hour,' Pollard replied.

'You must have made a quick run, Li.'

'We did. I started ten minutes after I received your telegram. I picked up the inspector at Scotland Yard, and we came by Taunton to Dulverton, and across Exmoor by the old coaching road. But where are Creed and Mr. Comstock? If they are in Lynmouth we must be careful that they don't — '

'They are not in Lynmouth, Li. Edgar Creed has gone on to Countisbury, and I dare say Cyrus B. Comstock is there, too.'

'Well, let me have your story. I had a visit from Hawke, but he could not give me a very clear account of what had happened. I understood that Creed got a bag from the cloakroom at Charing Cross Station.'

'Yes, that's right.'

The young man told in full of the events of the day, and related how he had shadowed the crook from the Hotel Majestic to Paddington.

'What do you make of it?' he continued. 'Do you think the rubies were in the bag?'

Crane shook his head.

'No, I don't,' he answered. 'I should say it was impossible. The bag must have been deposited at the cloakroom before George Harrap was murdered. The stones were most ingeniously concealed somewhere in Edgar Creed's flat, and he had them with him when he gave you the slip the other day, and went to Waterloo to meet Cyrus B. Comstock. Tonight they will change hands. The millionaire will buy them, and he will pay Creed a large price. He won't have them long, though. We will arrest both Comstock and the crook.'

'We will have to find them first, Li.'

'There won't be any difficulty about that. I have no doubt they are at the Blue Ball Inn at Countisbury. I know it well. It is a secluded little tavern, and just the place for a safe deal in stolen jewels. I want to survey the ground before we take any action. We will drive through Countisbury, leave the car on the open moor a couple of hundred yards beyond the Blue Ball, and walk back.'

Inspector Pidgeon shrugged his shoulders.

'Perhaps we'll be too late,' he said. 'The men may be on their way back to London by now.'

'I don't think so,' Crane replied. 'They probably intend to stay at the inn until morning. But we mustn't waste any time. Come along, Harry!' he added. 'Get in.'

The young man climbed to the rear seat of the car, and Crane drove slowly over the bridge, and up the lonely road that skirted precipitous cliffs, and led to Countisbury.

'I wonder,' he remarked, half to himself, 'if those rubies will cost any more lives before they are recovered?'

'They may,' said the inspector, 'unless we take Creed by surprise. He is a desperate man, Crane, and he will do some shooting if he gets a chance.'

★ ★ ★

It was not only for reasons of prudence that Cyrus B. Comstock had arranged to meet the crook in the secluded little village in the West Country. He was fond of the place. It was good for his health, and he was known there. On two occasions, while on a trip to England, he had stayed at Countisbury for several days, and fished for trout in the Exmoor streams.

Edgar Creed had no knowledge of North Devon, but the letter that had been left at the Hotel Majestic had given him full instructions, and Mr. Comstock had stated, in the letter, that he would be at the Blue Ball by the close of the day.

When Creed walked into the inn that night, however, a disappointment awaited him.

'My name is Hammond,' he said to the landlord. 'I am a friend of Mr. Cyrus Comstock.'

'Yes, I have been expecting you,' the man replied. 'I had a telegram from Mr. Comstock yesterday. He mentioned your name, and engaged three rooms. He hasn't arrived yet, though.'

'Not arrived? He should have been here some hours ago. What can have delayed him?'

'Perhaps his car broke down at some lonely spot, sir. I dare say he will get here before the night is over. Will you go up to his apartments? There are two bedrooms and a sitting room.'

'Yes, I will wait there.'

Half a dozen rustics, who were drinking beer in the taproom, gazed curiously at the stranger. Edgar Creed passed through, and followed the landlord to a comfortably-furnished little sitting room on the first floor.

He put his bag on the chair, and seated himself by a window from which he could see, by the dim light of the moon, an ancient church and some thatched cottages. It was very quiet and peaceful at this time of night. The inhabitants of Countisbury, two or three score in number, had gone to bed.

Creed was uneasy, and his apprehensions increased. It was possible, he felt, that Cyrus B. Comstock had taken alarm after leaving London, and concluded he would have nothing to do with the rubies.

'If the fellow plays me false,' he reflected, 'I'll find a way to be even with him.'

The night wore on, and finally, when

the crook had been waiting for the better part of an hour, he heard a throbbing sound in the direction of Lynmouth.

Two flaming lamps appeared, and a car stopped outside of the inn.

There were glimpses of two dusky figures. Soon afterwards footsteps ascended the stairs, and Mr. Comstock entered the sitting room. He was obviously in a very bad temper.

'Ah, here you are at last!' said Edgar Creed. 'I had almost given you up. What kept you so long?'

'That stupid servant of mine!' snapped Cyrus B. Comstock. 'He lost the way, for one thing, though I told him how to go. And then the car broke down in the wilds of Exmoor, and it took hours to repair it.'

'Well, it doesn't matter, now that you have arrived. I was afraid you were going to call the deal off.'

'I have a good mind to. I wish I had never laid eyes on you.'

'What do you mean by that? What's wrong?'

Mr. Comstock frowned.

'I can't help feeling worried,' he said. 'I

am running a big risk.'

'That's all nonsense!' Creed replied.
'There isn't the slightest risk.'

'How do you know? You admitted that you had been watched in London, and the police, or Lionel Crane, may have tracked you down here.'

'They could not possibly have done so. You can take my word for it.'

'What does your word count for? Can you swear that nobody was watching you on the two occasions when you called at my hotel?'

'I can swear to it.'

'Are you sure you were not followed from the Hotel Majestic to Paddington today?'

'I am certain I was not. I was on my guard all the time. It is a foolish idea you have got into your head. There is no reason whatever for you to feel uneasy. We are as safe here in this lonely inn as we would be on a desert island.'

'I'm not taking any chances, at all events,' said Mr. Comstock. 'The car is at the side of the road, in readiness for an immediate start. And Jupiter is out there on the watch, hiding in some bushes. We shall have a warning from him if — '

He paused, and glanced at the kitbag.

'You have the rubies there?' he inquired.

'Yes, they are in the bag,' Edgar Creed answered. 'I got it from the cloakroom at Charing Cross today.'

'And you were under surveillance, perhaps when you went there.'

'I know better, Mr. Comstock. Do you want to see the stones now?'

'No, not now. I will have something to eat first. You are hungry, I suppose?'

'Yes, I have had nothing since luncheon.'

Cyrus B. Comstock pulled a bell-cord. The landlord presently came in, and, having received an order, he withdrew, and returned shortly with a bottle of wine, and cold supper on a tray.

He laid the table and went out. Edgar Creed and Mr. Comstock seated themselves, and for a while they ate and drank in silence. Creed was on tenterhooks of anxiety. Though he had counted on returning to London a rich man, he was not so certain now that he would; for there was still, as he perceived, a shade of apprehension in the American's eyes.

When they had finished their supper Cyrus B. Comstock softly bolted the door, and stepping to the windows, one of which overlooked a garden at the side of the dwelling, he lowered the blinds.

'And now for the rubies,' he said, almost in a whisper. 'But I don't promise to buy them.'

'You won't refuse,' Edgar Creed replied. 'I'm not afraid of that.'

He unlocked and opened the kitbag, and, thrusting his hand beneath a heap of clothing, he produced a small parcel that was tied with cord and sealed with wax.

Having cut the wrapping away from it and disclosed to view a cardboard box, he raised the lid and took out a pouch of chamois leather. He held it up by the bottom, and the rubies rolled on to the table in a red, sparkling shower.

'There you are, sir!' he said.

Mr. Comstock stared breathlessly.

'What beauties!' he gasped. 'Ah, what beauties!'

He was in transports of delight. With flushed cheeks and dilated eyes, with twitching features, he gloated over the flaming, blazing, scintillating stones. He counted them, tossed them about, and clinked them together, the while he uttered low exclamations of rapture.

He handled them with trembling fingers, caressed them lovingly, fondled them, played with them as a child might play with coloured beads, or a miser with his hoarded gold. His ruling passion, the craze for rare jewels, was stirred to the depths.

'They are wonderful!' he murmured, with a quiver in his voice. 'Marvellous! You did not exaggerate the rarity and beauty of these stones Mr. Bradlaw! There can be none anywhere to compare with them! Not in the wide world! A man might sell his very soul to possess them! They will be the pride of my collection.'

'I knew how you would feel,' remarked Edgar Creed, who was now sure of striking a bargain.

Cyrus B. Comstock reluctantly replaced the rubies in the pouch, and as he put it down on the table he gave a quick start and turned pale.

'What was that?' he whispered. 'Did you hear it?'

'What do you mean?' Creed asked.

'I heard a rustling noise. I swear I did!'

'So did I. It was only the wind blowing the boughs of a tree against one of the windows.'

'Yes, I dare say you are right. If there was any danger Jupiter would have warned me. He is on the alert.'

There was a short silence, while the American pulled his shaken nerves together. Edgar Creed laughed contemptuously.

'It is nothing to laugh at,' said Mr. Comstock. 'I shall be glad to be back in London. We will leave presently. I won't spend the night here.'

'And the rubies?' Creed answered, 'You will buy them?'

'I can't refuse, risk or no risk.'

'You will pay my price, sir?'

'Yes, I will give you one hundred thousand pounds.'

'It must be in cash, Mr. Comstock.'

'Of course. A cheque drawn to your order would link my name with the transaction. But I can't give you the money at once. I shall have to get it from my New York bankers through a London bank. The matter can easily be arranged. I will meet you somewhere in London, at a safe place, in two or three days. And, meanwhile, I will retain possession of the stones. You can trust me. I am a man of my word, and you need not fear I will try to cheat you. You could denounce me to the police if I did.'

As Cyrus B. Comstock spoke, a shade of apprehension crept into his eyes again, and he gazed at the crook with knit brows.

'I have a poor memory sometimes,' he continued. 'Something which I had forgotten has just occurred to me. When I was at breakfast this morning in the dining room of the Hotel Majestic, I overheard part of a conversation between two gentlemen who were at the next table. They were talking of a man of the name of Harrap, who had been murdered a week ago in a train travelling from

Dover to Victoria, and one of them remarked to the other that, though there had been no mention of it in the papers, it was known to the police that the rubies stolen from the Mines of Mogok were in the dead man's possession, and they were the motive for the murder.'

Edgar Creed's heart sank. What was coming next? Was the bargain going to fall through, he wondered? Should he lie? No, he had better brazen it out, and trust to the American's cupidity.

'What you heard was true,' he calmly assented.

'It must have been you, then, who murdered the man Harrap!' declared Mr. Comstock.

'I did, sir.'

'And you stole the rubies from him?'

'Yes, I knew he had them. At the time they were in the registered parcel you saw me open. Harrap had sent them to Dover for safe keeping, addressed in an assumed name, and he had been down there that day to claim the parcel at the post office.'

Cyrus B. Comstock shook his head. He was genuinely horrified. He glanced wistfully at the chamois-leather pouch, and looked at the crook as if he was in dread of him.

'I wish I had known this before,' he said, in an indignant tone. 'What am I to do about it? These stones are stained with blood and I have been on the point of purchasing them from a red-handed murderer!'

'Take them or leave them!' Edgar Creed sullenly replied. 'Please yourself.'

Mr. Comstock hesitated. Once more he was struggling between desire and scruples. He could not decide what to do.

'Was it on the night of the murder,' he asked, after a brief pause, 'that Lionel Crane searched your flat in Cecil Buildings?'

'It was on the same night,' Creed answered.

'Then he suspected that you had the rubies?' said Mr. Comstock.

'It appeared that he did, though I had believed otherwise.'

'And he must have tracked you from Victoria to the Charing Cross Road.'

'No, he couldn't have done that. He

came to my place merely on suspicion. To be candid, he knew I had been trying to find Harrap with the intention of robbing him of the rubies.'

'How is it,' Mr. Comstock resumed, 'that Lionel Crane failed to discover the stones when he made the search?'

Edgar Creed smiled.

'I tricked him neatly,' he said. 'I will tell you all about it, and your mind will be relieved if you are still uneasy. I was not in the least suspicious of danger when I got to my flat that night, but, none the less, I was anxious to be rid of the rubies for a time, and I hit on a clever scheme for doing so. I thought it advisable, however, to alter my appearance, and with some touches of greasepaint, and the aid of a large false moustache, I transformed myself into the very double of a retired colonel who lived on the floor above me.

'I put the registered parcel and some clothes into the kitbag, descended the stairs, and walked out of the building under the very nose of the hall porter. I took a taxi and drove to Charing Cross

Station, deposited the bag at the cloak-room, and drove back to my flat in another taxi. And it was no great while afterwards that Lionel Crane arrived with his partner, Pollard, and a couple of Scotland Yard men. I enjoyed the search. It was highly amusing, Mr. Comstock. They gave it up in the end, and politely withdrew.'

'They searched you personally, I suppose?'

'From head to foot, sir.'

'And they didn't find the receipt for the bag?'

'No, they overlooked it. I had fortu-nately concealed it inside one of my socks.'

'If Lionel Crane suspected that you had the rubies,' said Mr. Comstock, 'he must have also suspected that it was you who murdered the man Harrap.'

'It makes no difference if he did,' Creed replied.

'No difference? Unless Lionel Crane is a fool — and he is far from that — he would have kept you under surveillance since the night of the murder. I strongly believe that he did. He may be lurking about somewhere outside now.'

'It is impossible. He is a couple of hundred miles away, in London. You can be sure of that.'

Cyrus B. Comstock was doubtful, after what he had been told. He glanced again at the chamois-leather pouch, and resolutely averted his eyes from it. He had been led to change his mind.

'You can keep the rubies,' he said. 'I won't have anything to do with them, Mr. Bradlaw. I mean it. It will be useless for you to — '

He broke off abruptly, and sprang to his feet, the colour ebbing from his face, his limbs trembling. He had just heard, at no great distance, the hooting of an owl. As he listened it was repeated.

'What's the matter?' asked Creed.

'That's my servant Jupiter!' gasped Mr. Comstock. 'The signal I arranged with him. We are in danger! Lionel Crane must be out there. And probably the police as well.'

His terror was real, but Edgar Creed, who had risen from his chair with fury in his eyes, thought otherwise. It was inconceivable to him that he could have been traced from London to this remote spot in North Devon.

'You treacherous hound!' he cried. 'You have played me false! You told the police I had the rubies, and lured me down here to be arrested. I see it all. Curse you! By heavens, I've a good mind to — '

As he spoke he let fly with his fist, and Cyrus B. Comstock, struck on the point of the jaw, went crashing to the floor, and lay there like a log.

Creed snatched the pouch of rubies from the table and slipped them into his pocket; then dashed to the nearest window, tore the blind from its fastenings, and threw the casement open.

Below him was the garden at the side of the inn. He swung himself out, clutching the windowsill, and let go. And the next instant there was a startled exclamation, followed by the sound of a heavy fall.

17

The Curse of the Rubies Again

Pollard had been perched precariously beneath the window, clinging to the thick growth of ivy that clothed the wall, for some little time. The greater part of the conversation within the room had clearly reached his ears, and he was hastily descending, after hearing Mr. Comstock knocked down, when Edgar Creed dropped on top of him, and broke his hold of the ivy.

They fell together, and landed in a clump of bushes, which saved him from serious injury.

Pollard lay motionless, bruised and dazed by the fall; while Creed, who was not in the least hurt, scrambled to his feet, and sped towards a gate that opened on to the road.

The American's car was standing there, in front of the Blue Ball, and he hoped to be able to escape in it. But a glimpse of two dusky figures — they were Crane and Inspector Pidgeon — warned the crook that he must abandon his intention.

Without an instant's delay, he whipped round, and with pistols cracking behind him, and bullets humming by his ears, he dashed to the rear end of the garden, and with an agile leap vaulted over a low hedge.

He was at the borders of the village now. There were no cottages beyond him. He had no idea of his bearings, and he did not stop to consider. All he knew was that he was on the edge of the wild, lonely waste of Exmoor Forest.

Taking to his heels, he ran blindly, aimlessly, and presently stumbled on a road. He held to this, and when he had gone for a few yards he came to a big car that was deserted, and had its lamps extinguished.

'Ah, here's a stroke of luck!' he murmured. 'This must be Lionel Crane's car!'

As yet there were no sounds of pursuit. All was quiet in the direction of the village, much to Creed's relief. He could hear the clumping of hoofs in the opposite direction, however; and when he had cranked up the engine he climbed to the front seat of the car and waited. A farmer, mounted on a horse, was approaching, and as he drew near the crook called to him.

'Where does this road go to?' he asked.

'It goes eighteen mile over Exmoor to Porlock and Minehead, zur,' the farmer replied, reining in his steed.

'Minehead — eh? I suppose there's a railway station and a telegraph office there?'

'Oh, yes, zur!'

'Can't I get across the moor in any other direction?'

'Not this side of Porlock, zur. You might beyond there, but I doubt it. I'm not sure if there is a road or not, and if there is one you would find it rough going.'

'Thank you, my good fellow!'

The farmer jogged on his way, wondering what the stranger was doing here at this hour; and Edgar Creed started off at once, sending the big car spinning into the moonlit night. He must go by Porlock and Minehead, even at the risk of being intercepted by a telegraph message. There was no help for it.

He was in a savage mood. Satisfied that the young man he had dropped on to from the window was Pollard, he had no doubt Lionel Crane also had been in the vicinity. And he was afraid he had one or two Scotland Yard men with him.

'Curse the luck!' he said to himself.

'And curse that dirty dog Comstock! I wish I had killed him. Will Crane come after me at once in the American's car, I wonder? Or will he delay to send a telegram from Lynmouth to the police at Minehead? There is no telling which. I have a good start, at all events. If only I can keep in the lead. And if the petrol doesn't run out.'

It was not likely, he felt, that Crane would delay. He anticipated a prompt pursuit, and his fears were soon verified. He frequently looked back, and at length he saw, far behind him, the flaming lamps of a car. Lionel Crane and his companions were already giving chase.

And now, though he was a man of dogged, tenacious courage, Creed's iron nerve almost failed him. It was about the tightest place he had ever been in, and he was badly frightened.

What if he should be caught? The very thought terrified him, and he shuddered as a ghastly vision of the gallows rose in his mind. Arrest would mean hanging, for he had the rubies with him, the proof that it was he who had murdered George Harrap.

Should he get rid of his plunder, the jewels he had shed blood to acquire? No, he would cling to them, keep them to the last. Why not? If he were to throw them away, he reflected, it would not save him from the scaffold, for Cyrus Comstock was alive, and he would tell the whole story.

'If they corner me I'll fight for it,' he muttered, with an oath, as he looked at his automatic to be sure it was fully loaded. 'I had rather be shot than arrested.'

County Gate, the borderline between

Devon and Somerset, had already been passed. The miles reeled by. His cheeks stung by the fleet air, his lips tight-set, and his eyes scanning the road, Edgar Creed drove on and on over the high ground that was like a Roman causeway on a titanic scale.

From the left of the coast hill, where the Bristol Channel lay deep, floated on the breeze the salty tang of the sea. Off to the right the ancient domain of Exmoor, bathed in the milky glow of the moon, rolled northward in great undulations, in a haze of opalescent colouring, to the far horizon.

So the chase continued, and, meanwhile, the blazing lamps of the pursuing car — it was more powerful than the one the crook was driving — crept steadily closer and closer.

Yearnor Moor Stables, on a wooded part of the moor, flashed by in a blur. The woods dwindled, and when Creed emerged from them, on to a vast stretch of open ground, where grew only heather and stunted bushes, Crane and his companions were within less than two hundred yards, and were still gaining.

In desperation, Creed used his automatic now. The sharp reports rang on the night, waking the echoes, while he gripped the wheel with one hand, and fired with the other as often as he looked back.

He fired again and again, and the pursuers replied with a straggling volley of pistol-shots. Nobody was hit. No tyres were burst.

Creed had no spare cartridges, and when at length his weapon was empty he had got to the top of Porlock Hill, one of the steepest and most dangerous hills in the West Country.

He perceived the danger, and abated his speed. Yet he descended recklessly enough, and narrowly escaped a smash at the bottom.

He safely navigated the sharp turn, however, swerving to the left with a margin of a couple of inches; and putting on full speed again, he raced down the remainder of the hill, between a few cottages, to the entrance to the quaint little main street of Porlock village. He had another turn to make, and here disaster awaited him.

'Curse you, Crane!' he shouted. 'You won't take me alive!'

They were his last words, and they were true ones. As he spoke the car swung dizzily round, plunged at a hedge, and recoiled from it; then, spinning in a half circle on two wheels, it dived into a stone wall, and overturned with a rending, shattering crash.

When the pursuing car reached the spot a few moments later, and Lionel Crane stepped out of it with Inspector Pidgeon and Pollard, the startled villagers were swarming from their houses, and a shrill clamour was ringing. The wrecked car was on fire, blazing furiously, and Edgar Creed was lying clear of it at the edge of the road.

'He must have been killed, Li!' exclaimed Pollard.

Crane knelt by the prostrate figure.

'Yes, he is dead,' he declared, as he took the pouch of rubies from one of the crook's pockets. 'He has broken his neck.'

The fatal curse of the rubies again! The sinister jewels, seemingly endowed with evil powers, had claimed another human life. And with the exception of Neil Allison and Leonard Drewitt, each of the victims of the curse had acquired the stones dishonestly, and had richly deserved his fate.

'It is a pity,' said the inspector. 'I wanted to see this scoundrel Creed hanged.'

'He has cheated the gallows,' Crane replied, 'and gone before a higher tribunal than the law to be judged.'

A crowd of excited people had gathered at the scene of the disaster, and amongst them was the village constable. Having disclosed his identity to the man, Crane gave him a brief explanation of what had occurred, told him to have the body of Edgar Creed removed to the Ship Inn nearby, and promised to return to Porlock the next day.

And shortly afterwards, when nothing was left of the wrecked car but a heap of charred and twisted metal, he set off for Countisbury with his companions in the American's car. His task was not finished yet. He had another stern duty to perform.

18

Mr. Comstock Has A Bad
Quarter of an Hour

At a late hour that night, as it was drawing near to morning, Cyrus B. Comstock was alone in his sitting room at the Blue Ball, at Countisbury, huddled limply in a big chair, and nursing a bruised jaw. And Jupiter, the valet, was down in the taproom, trying to make a number of curious villagers believe that he had no knowledge of what had happened.

The American millionaire was virtually a prisoner. Crane had instructed the landlord of the inn not to allow him to depart under any circumstances, and Mr. Comstock was well aware of the fact.

Knowing as he did that it was a serious crime to purchase stolen property, he was in a state of trepidation, wondering what his punishment would be. He had been waiting in suspense for hours, racking his brains for some means of getting out of the scrape he was in.

But he was not a coward, this millionaire whose wealth had helped him to evade the law in his own country; and when at length he heard a car arrive, and knew the detective he dreaded had returned, he braced himself for the ordeal.

He sat erect, and listened. There were footsteps on the stairs. The door was opened and Lionel Crane came into the room with Inspector Pidgeon and Pollard. His face was cold and stern.

'I have recovered the rubies,' he said, his eyes bent on the American 'By what name did you know the man who had them?'

'He told me his name was Bradlaw,' Mr. Comstock replied.

'He lied to you. His real name was Edgar Creed, and he was a notorious crook. He is dead. The car was overturned at the village of Porlock, across the moor, and he was instantly killed. I am here now to reckon with you.'

'I have done nothing wrong, sir.'

'Nothing wrong?' Crane angrily repeated. 'Don't try to deceive me, or it will be the worse for you. It will surprise you, perhaps, to learn that you have been under constant surveillance from the time you arrived at Waterloo Station until you left the Hotel Majestic for the West Country. Edgar Creed has also been watched, and he was followed from Paddington yesterday afternoon.'

'It is to your credit, sir,' said Cyrus B. Comstock, 'that you have done such clever work. I honestly congratulate you.'

'No compliments, if you please. Not from you. I have a great deal of knowledge of you, as it happens. Your record in New York has been none too clean. You have been unscrupulous in your methods of acquiring jewels for your famous collection, and you came down to Countisbury with the intention of purchasing the rubies from Edgar Creed. You had him meet you at this lonely place because you were afraid to have dealings with him in London.'

'I won't deny it, Mr. Crane. I can

assure you, though — '

'Pray let me finish. You knew, of course, that you were engaged in a criminal enterprise.'

'It would have been a crime if I had carried it out, sir.'

'You would have done so had not circumstances prevented you. I presume you knew that the rubies had been stolen from the Mines of Mogok, in Upper Burma.'

'I was aware of that, I will admit.'

'Did you know that Edgar Creed had committed murder to get possession of them?' Crane continued.

'Yes, I did,' Mr. Comstock assented. 'I had my suspicions of the man. I questioned him closely, and compelled him to make a clean breast of it.'

'He confessed, then? And you, knowing him to be a murderer, would have dealt with him?'

'You are wrong, sir. You are under a misapprehension. I am not as bad as you think I am.'

'Don't make excuses. You have played the part of a scoundrel. You are liable to a term of imprisonment, and it is my duty to have you arrested.'

Cyrus B. Comstock turned very pale.

'I repeat that you are under a wrong impression,' he said, looking the detective straight in the eyes. 'I will tell you the truth, the whole truth, and only the truth. I was tempted. I wanted the rubies badly, and I might have been unscrupulous enough to buy them in the end. From the first I was afraid, though. I wavered between desire and fear, and when I learned that Edgar Creed was a murderer — it was not until tonight, in this room, that he admitted the fact — I changed my mind. I told him flatly that I would have nothing to do with the stones, and that is why he jumped up in a rage, and struck me. It is the truth, whether you believe me or not. I swear it is.'

Pollard glanced at Crane.

'That's quite right, Li,' he said. 'The deal was off. I can vouch for it.'

Crane hesitated. He could not at once make up his mind what to do. He was influenced by two things, however. He knew, for one thing, that at the last Mr.

Comstock had refused to purchase the rubies. And in the second place, he doubted if it would be possible to convict the American should a charge be brought against him.

'You richly deserve to be punished,' he said, after brief consideration. 'But on one condition, sir, I will deal leniently with you.'

Mr. Comstock's gloomy face brightened a little.

'What is it?' he asked.

'You will go free if you will present the sum of one hundred thousand pounds to some charity which I will name later.'

'I will do so with pleasure. And with gratitude to you.'

'Very well,' said Crane. 'That is understood. For the present you will remain here. When I return to London you will accompany me, and you will stay at the Hotel Majestic until the matter has been arranged.

'And I trust that in future, Mr. Comstock,' he added, as he turned to the door, 'you will not let your passion for jewels tempt you to any dishonest transactions. You have had a severe lesson. Profit by it!'

* * *

For several days vivid accounts of the sensational case of the Burmese rubies, and the bloodshed they had indirectly been the cause of, appeared in the newspapers. No mention was made of Cyrus B. Comstock, however. He gladly fulfilled his promise. He gave Lionel Crane a cheque for one hundred thousand pounds, and, a sadder and a wiser man, he sailed for New York.

The rubies were handed over to the manager of the company's London offices, and the reward which had been offered for their recovery was paid to Crane, who kept just enough of it to recoup him for his expenses and the car he had lost, and shared the remainder between the Scotland Yard men who had assisted him, and the widow of Leonard Drewitt.

Mr. Malcolm Graeme was reinstated in his position, and shortly afterwards he departed for Burma with his daughter Mary. Crane saw them off from Victoria, on their way to Marseilles to catch a P. and O. Liner; and as he left the station Malcolm Graeme's parting words were in his mind:

'I am going back to the beautiful tropical land where my heart is. Back to the green jungles, and the pagodas, and the tinkly temple bells. Back to the romance of the East. And back to the work I love. And that I am a happy man again is due to you, Mr. Crane. I may never see you again, but night and day you will be in m⋯⋯⋯⋯ ng as I live I shall ⋯⋯⋯ epest gratitude what ⋯⋯⋯ e.'